Praise for *One*

"With its prickly (but lovable) heroine, tongue-in-cheek look at conventions, and genuinely heartwarming romance, *One Con Glory* has it all. Sarah Kuhn's tale of emotional realization, of a childhood hero lost and found—sprinkled throughout with a healthy dose of pop geekery—is not to be missed."
—The Book Smugglers
thebooksmugglers.com

"I started laughing two pages into this book, and did not stop, although by the end I was also interjecting adoring coos… *One Con Glory* is sharp, witty, well-paced, feminist geek girl good times."
—Karen Healey, author of *Guardian of the Dead*

"Funny, sharp, and charming, Sarah Kuhn's *One Con Glory* is as smart as it is smart-assed: not only is it fluent in geek-speak, it knows we've got more issues than just the ones in our longboxes. *One Con Glory* bears approximately the same relation to chick-lit novels that *Spaced* does to sitcoms: it is (to quote from the *Six Million Dollar Man* opening) better, stronger, faster. A frakkin' fun read from a writer to watch out for."
—Jeff Lester, The Savage Critics
savagecritic.com

"The characters of *One Con Glory* are believable without straying into blatant stereotypes of the variety of geeks out there. You know these guys; they're your friends, your neighbors, your raiding party. The journey Julie makes over the course of the story is remarkable and Kuhn makes it easy to fall in love with them all… Hollywood needs to option this NOW."
—Jill Pantozzi, The Nerdy Bird
TheNerdyBird.com

"A surprising love story populated with unusual but endearing characters you can easily imagine meeting on the comics convention circuit. It's like *Notting Hill* with cosplay. Also, Julie is totally right about Scott and Jean."
—Caroline Pruett, Fantastic Fangirls
fantasticfangirls.org

This book is a work of fiction. Names, characters, places, and incidents are products of the author's imagination or are used fictitiously. Any resemblance to actual events or persons, living or dead, is entirely coincidental.

ISBN: 978-0-578-06075-0

First Alert Nerd Press Edition: November 2009

Visit Alert Nerd:
alertnerd.com
alertnerdpress.com

Printed in the United States by Lulu.com.

SARAH KUHN

ALERT NERD PRESS

– PART I –
PON FARR

The Three Glories

January 14, 2009

By the time I was sixteen, I had already gone through three Glory Gilmores. She was six inches of garishly painted plastic with thirty-one points of articulation, the queen of my action figure kingdom. And yet, she kept getting lost.

Original Glory was a victim of the neighbors' dog, her head gouged with teeth marks and drowned in slobber. I hated that fucking dog.

Glory II was slaughtered during one of Melissa Perkins' infamous fourth-grade recess rampages. Melissa—playground enforcer and Laura Ashley-swathed devil spawn—spotted an opening when Glory fell out of my pocket during an extended run on the monkey bars. Her massive Mary Jane crushed those plastic limbs to smithereens.

Glory the Third...oh, this is a sad one. Andy Oppenheimer, who was second chair to my first chair clarinet, gave me Glory the Third for my fifteenth birthday after hearing about the untimely demises of Glories I and II (we had a lot of time on our hands because the band director was always trying to get the goddamn trombone section in tune). Now that I look back on it, I think maybe he liked me a little bit. Unfortunately, I was going through a rather short-lived phase of "maturity" and donated my entire action figure collection to Goodwill. I only hope Glory the Third ended up in a good home.

Of course, there was one final Glory...The Last Glory. When I lost her, it was due to one thing and one thing only: my own excruciating stupidity.

I only hope that someday she'll find it in her heart to come back to me.

—*Posted on GloryGilmoreLives.com*

February 25, 2002
10:34 a.m.

Curtis is kind of a douchebag.

I mean, we both like Pad Thai and scouring used bookstores for beat-up sci-fi paperbacks and that episode of *Star Trek: The Next Generation* where Picard learns how to play the Ressikan flute.

But then he has to go and do all this douchebaggy shit, like telling anyone who will listen about his "male feminism." Or bragging that he can play three whole chords on the guitar, when I know for a fucking fact he's only mastered two.

These are probably not the thoughts I should be thinking when Curtis is on top of me.

I squint up at his mottled face, which is screwed into an expression of pure...lust? No. More like concentration. Sweat beads his flushed brow, his thatch of dyed-black hair flopping up and down, up and down as he pumps away.

"Oh...oh...god...dess!" he gasps. Pump, pump, pump.

Do you see what I mean? Who does that? Who says "oh, goddess" during sex? Well, okay—maybe people who, you know, worship actual goddesses as part of their religion. But Curtis doesn't identify as, like, "pagan." He's just a fucking poser.

I arrange my expression into a similar concentration-posing-as-lust sort of shape and try to meet his eyes. Maybe that will help speed the, ahem, process along.

Pump, pump, pump.

Or...it will just make me feel like we're engaged in a really weird staring contest. I allow my gaze to drift to the left of Curtis' head, eyes scanning my hovelicious dorm room. CDs in their milk-crate homes,

Tetrised into submission. Candy-colored iMac lazily repeating its generic screensaver, as if shooting off pixely fireworks is a big pain in its nonexistent ass. Long shelf of action figures affixed precariously to the wall, Buffy Summers rubbing elbows with Dana Scully and Spock. All of them arranged in a way that makes perfect sense to me. All of them—*wait a second.*

I crane my neck, trying to see around Curtis' bobbing head. Unfortunately, he keeps bobbing into the spot I'm trying to focus on.

Bob—quick, look!

Bob—is that really...ugh. Can't...see. I strain just a little bit farther.

Bob. What the...

"God...DESS!" Curtis pants. And honestly, that is fucking *it.*

"Enough!" I growl. I shove him off me, putting all my muscle into it. The fact that he maintains an emaciated indie-rocker physique of roughly ninety-five pounds helps things along.

"Wha..." Curtis attempts to clutch a corner of sheet, but he's a split second too late, and goes tumbling off the edge of my narrow twin bed, landing on the ground with a solid "thump."

"Owwwwwwwwwww!" he yelps, throwing me a look of injured contempt.

Ignoring him, I pull the sheet around me like a makeshift toga and stride up to the toy shelf, eyes glued to the spot that has captured my attention.

"Why?" I mutter, almost to myself. "Why...is Tigra mixed in with the classic Avengers?"

I whirl around and frown at Curtis, eyes narrowing to tiny slits. He's making a big show of checking himself for broken bones. Whatever. The floor isn't *that* hard.

He looks up at me and cocks his head to the side, dazed and naked. "What?"

I flap my hand at the shelf. "Tigra didn't join the Avengers 'til the '80s," I say. "She should be over *here,* with She-Hulk and Captain Marvel." I gently slide Tigra's muscular orange form to the correct place. Then I train my patented death stare on Curtis. "You moved her."

He spreads his hands out, palms up, beseeching. "Babe. I still don't know what you're talking about."

Ugh. I hate that nickname. He *knows* I hate that nickname. And nicknames of any kind, really.

I cross the room in two steps and stand over him, glowering. "You. Moved. Her."

Curtis brushes his lank forelock out of his eyes, pursing his lips the tiniest bit. He contorts his spindly, so-white-it's-almost-translucent form into a hip-jutting, come-hither pose. "Wow," he says, his voice husky. "You're so *hot* when you're mad. Why don't we get back to—"

"I told you not to touch my shit," I snap.

He frowns, all traces of ill-conceived bedroom eyes dropping away. "Fine," he says peevishly. "I moved Ladytiger—"

"*Tigra.*"

"Whatever." He glares at me, the pieces of his usual cooler-than-thou armor snapping firmly into place. "I wanted to see if you would notice."

I tighten my grip on the sheet-toga. "Well, go you, I totally did. Now what?"

He scrambles to his feet, clamping his hands on his bony hips. "Now?!" he says incredulously. "Now I have confirmation of what a crazy bitch you are!"

"You're moving my stuff around as some kind of bizarre psychology experiment and *I'm* the crazy one?"

He takes a step, closing the space between us so that we're nose to nose. "You," he says, jabbing the air with his spindly index finger, "would rather obsess over Tiger-Girl—"

"Tigra!"

"—than fuck!"

I raise an eyebrow. "I would rather obsess over a lot of things than fuck *you.*"

Our gazes lock and we face off for a few weighted moments, breath coming and going in furious gasps, red-hot fury barely contained. If this were a shitty romantic comedy—you know, one of the ones where the woman learns an Important Lesson About Not Being Uptight—this would be the part where we start making out like crazy, our mutual hatred a mere mask for the passion lurking underneath.

Instead, Curtis lunges forward, shoves me out of the way, and snatches a six-inch piece of plastic off the toy shelf.

"What...Curtis!" I yelp.

But it's too late. He's out the door, running like hell, dick flapping frantically back and forth like a lily-white flag of surrender.

"*Fuck.*"

Gathering my sheet around me, I bolt after him, chasing his naked form down the too-long dorm hall. He holds his stolen prize aloft, and I can see that she's black and red and garish as all get out and...oh my God. He didn't. Not *her*.

"Goddammit," I mutter. "That's my *fourth one*."

"Fuck you, Julie!" he screams. "Comic books are a TOOL OF THE PATRIARCHY!"

I increase my speed, bare feet slapping against the threadbare institutional carpet, worn down to almost nothing after being tread on by decades of graceless college students.

Curtis reaches the end of the hall and throws open the double doors, sunlight illuminating his scrawny body.

"He wouldn't," I growl.

He does. Curtis bursts through the doors and into the outside world.

I follow, but my moment's hesitation costs me. As I stumble down the rough concrete steps, I see him streaking into the distance, a tiny white dot blipping across campus, like a beacon on a radar screen. A beacon representing douchebag boyfriends—well, douchebag ex-boyfriends, because *we are so broken up now*—everywhere.

Huffing and puffing, I fall to my knees, dew-drenched grass soaking the sheet that is still, improbably, wrapped around me.

"Asshole," I mutter into the empty air.

July 17, 2009
8:46 in the fucking morning.

The food court hurts my eyes. And my nose. And my…general sense of decency.

Let's be real: the food court hurts *everything*.

Especially when it's 8:46 in the fucking morning and my best friend is trying to convince me that tater tots make for a balanced breakfast.

"You know you want it."

Mitch Caplan waves a deep-fried glob of starch under my nose, a devilish grin playing across his broad, freckle-specked face. Shuddering, I bat his hand away.

8:47 now. Thirteen more minutes in this fragrant, brightly lit haven of over-processed foodlike objects. I fidget in my rickety plastic chair, trying to block out sight and smell and sound.

"—because you're never guaranteed a good crispiness level with french fry breading, but those McDonald's hash brown thingies are almost *too much* with the crunch. Am I right? Are you even listening to me?"

"What? I mean…yes." I shift around so I'm facing Mitch and widen my eyes into a passable expression of true attentiveness. He grins and pops another tot in his mouth.

"You are so not listening," he says through a mouthful of golden-brown greaseball. "What's wrong, Julie? GinormoCon anticipation killin' ya dead?"

Before I can retort, a nasal voice cuts through the hazy, lard-scented air. "She's got stuff on her mind, Mitchell. Suckin' up to nerdlebrities is a lot of frakkin' work."

Our heads turn and there he is, an amalgam of pasty skin and beanpole limbs and pure smugginess. I narrow my eyes as he slides into a vacant seat at our minuscule table. "Braidbeard," I mutter. More of a tossed-off epithet than an actual greeting.

"How do you do that?" marvels Mitch. "It's like you just...appear. Out of nowhere."

Braidbeard swipes a tater tot and stuffs it in his mouth. "I have superpowers or whatever."

Right. Because arguing about DC continuity holes 'til you're blue in the face is a superpower now.

The source of his nickname—a scraggly beard, carefully arranged into three unkempt braids—dances back and forth as he chomps on the pilfered tot. "Double-u tee eff with that chick they just hired on *Powers That Be?*" he brays, eyes goggling behind his aggressively hip clunky glasses. "Are they actively trying to get cancelled? Because she's what I like to call a *show-killer*."

I groan and slump back in my seat, scanning the food court. Save for a trio of fresh-faced Skrulls huddled over a plate of nachos, we are apparently the only ones who felt the need to stake out the L.A. Convention Center minutes—nine minutes!—before the GinormoCon doors open.

I was hoping to avoid any and all classic Braidbeard dissertations on Why Everything Sucks today, but that's what I get for hanging out with Mitch. The boys work together at the entertainment website CinePlanet.com, writing quickie reviews and reporting on "exclusive" news bits. Perhaps sensing that being co-workers = forced camaraderie, Braidbeard leeches onto Mitch every chance he gets. And Mitch—a genial, 6'2" mountain of a man who projects an uncomplicated sort of goodwill—lets him.

"*Powers* was fucked as soon as they decided to retcon season three out of existence," Mitch says mildly.

I sneak a peek at my watch. Seven minutes. Mitch raises an eyebrow. "Seriously, why are you so antsy?" he asks. "I know Los Angeles' annual assemblage of all things geeky is exciting, but it ain't *that* exciting. And you have done this before."

I have. In fact, as a writer for the ever-shrinking genre-focused glossy *Mammoth Media*, I have covered GinormoCon, UnCon, CrappywasheddupcelebssigningshitformoneyCon, and the granddaddy—San Diego Comic-Con. I met Mitch and Braidbeard four years ago on this incestuous circuit: a motley trio of baby hack-reporters, our plastic-encased press badges stamped proudly on our chests like gleaming beacons of newbieness. Upon realizing that we all call San Francisco home, I started hanging out with them in non-con environments. Or with Mitch, anyway.

Now, I cradle my badge discreetly in my palm, absently running my thumb over the cheap, synthetic material.

This con is different. For a few reasons. For one very important reason. But I'm not going to tell them that.

"I just...I have this one-on-one later," I say. "And I'm kind of not into it."

"Oh?" says Mitch. "With who?"

My eyeballs wander over to the Skrulls. One of them has dribbled nacho cheese on his purple spandex uniform. I tip my head back and stare up at the impossibly high ceiling. "Jack Camden."

Mitch makes a spluttery sort of sound. "You?!" he chokes out. "*You're* interviewing Jack Camden? As in *Periodic Seven* leading man Jack Camden?"

Braidbeard's eyebrows knit together, forming a hairy caterpillar bridge. "I don't get it," he says. "Shouldn't Julie be doing girly little cartwheels over that guy?" He claps a hand over his heart and approximates what he probably imagines is a sound of womanly ecstasy. It sounds more like a badly injured parrot. "Soooooo dreeaaamy!" he trills in an offensively high-pitched "girl" voice. "Better than Edward Cullen!"

"How do you know who Edward Cullen is, B?" Mitch interjects. "I thought you refused to acknowledge *Twilight* because it—and I quote—'encourages little girls and soccer moms to invade our genre safe space.'"

"I love how that's the same 'safe space' that contains mega-booby Top Cow heroines," I mutter.

"Emo vamp's name is part of the POPULAR CULTURE," Braidbeard snits. "And popular culture is *my job*. Now tell me what the frak is up with Jack Camden."

I contemplate the ceiling for a moment more. Fucking Jack Camden. In truth, having to do this interview isn't *that* much of a hardship. It means my Bay Area-to-LAX plane ticket was paid for in full. It means I get to be at this con. And hopefully, *that* means I get to have my Big, Epic Moment later on.

"Alright, alright," says Mitch. "But please remember this when Julie is knee-deep in her tirade: you asked."

He did, didn't he? My head snaps back to an upright position. Across the room, the messy Skrull blots his uniform with a Shout wipe. I surreptitiously glance at my watch—8:55. Five minutes. Plenty of time to spit out my well-worn theory on why the existence of a B-list TV star is representative of everything that's wrong with popular culture. And, you know, *the world*.

"Look," I say, *"The Periodic Seven* is almost a perfect show, right? It's got those neat little plot twists, just the right amount of non-smirky irreverence, and a decent shot of old-fashioned cloak and daggery."

Braidbeard frowns. "What's a daggery?"

"Shhhh," says Mitch, lobbing the last soggy tater tot at him.

"It's reasonably faithful to the source material and the cast is pretty great," I continue. "Except for Camden. He's the one sour note. The Dazzler of the Marvel Universe, the Clooney of the Batman franchise—"

"Dazzler is a *highly underrated* character!" interrupts Braidbeard.

"The point is," I say, determined not to let him distract me from my closing thesis, "casting Jack Camden as Travis Trent is about ten billion different kinds of wrong. Travis is a scientist—a nerd—who just happens to be a superhero. Camden is a pretty boy who skates by on his cheekbones and has somehow managed to prolong a career that previously consisted solely of looking moderately conflicted in bad teen-romance flicks. He has no soul."

Grinning indulgently, Mitch choruses the final line with me: "And Travis Trent is supposed to have *soul*."

Braidbeard's eyes narrow. "I must admit to a certain…grudging admiration for your complete and utter obsession bordering on psychosis," he says. "But it's not like the source material was frakking Batman. Like, ten people read the original comic."

"She was one of 'em," says Mitch, jerking his chin in my direction. "You know, Julie, I've always thought this was a black mark on your otherwise impeccable taste."

"Yeah, yeah," I say. "I know it wasn't exactly Marvel's finest work to come out of the late '80s—"

"Third-tier *at best!*" shrieks Braidbeard.

"But if you go back and actually read it, all the stuff that makes the show great is there. Young scientists gain superpowers when their lab is hit by a chemical explosion and awesomeness ensues. And then there's Glory Gilmore."

"*Whoa.*" Braidbeard waves a pointy finger under my nose. "You are not dissing Dazzler and then holding Glory frakking Gilmore up as some kind of geek sacred cow."

"I always felt a connection to her," I say firmly. "Go back and read the comics—she's pretty fucking amazing."

"Dude...dude. Do you even remember what her stupid powers were?" Mitch throws back his head and roars with laughter. The effect is not unlike Sabretooth baring his massive fangs. "Shitty Jean Grey rip-off alert: Biokinesis and...something with telepathy?"

"Biokinesis and psychoempathy," I say through gritted teeth.

"Oh, right, so basically she could only move, like, *living* things and she could sense your emotions if you were standing right next to her." Mitch starts roaring again. "She was an even lamer version of Counselor Troi."

"I sense danger...AND HACKY PLOTLINES!" Braidbeard is practically aerobicizing out of his chair.

"But I'll give you this," says Mitch. "TV Glory? Claire Yardley? She's pretty good."

"*Yeah*, she is," Braidbeard leers. "She's got at least two pretty incredible, um, assets. If you know what I'm saying."

I sigh and slump back in my seat. Whatever. Ever since *The Periodic Seven* was reinvented as a TV series, geeks have gained a new appreciation for Glory...or for this version of Glory, anyway.

"I meant her boobs."

"We got it, B."

I like Claire—I do. But Comic Book Glory...Comic Book Glory is the *true* Glory. Comic Book Glory is the one I felt close to. Like me, she had a strangely voluminous mane of jet-black hair that was neither wavy nor straight, but somewhere in between. Also like me, she tended to be in a constant state of annoyance about *something*. As an overly morose seven-year-old, I got really crabby when, say, my mom wouldn't let me wear my kick-ass red high-tops every single day. Comic Book Glory, meanwhile, was always getting pissed at her teammates for making various mutant messes around the Periodic Seven HQ. Only when Glory got pissed, she could throw your ass against the wall *with her mind*.

Which I wouldn't mind doing to my con companions right about now.

But then Mitch is jumping up, gathering his things, and tossing the cardboard tater tot container into the garbage. "Doors are open!" he cries. "Let's go!"

Nine o'clock. Zero minutes.

Bring on the epicness.

After a whirlwind morning of panels and roundtable interviews, I'm starving and slightly woozy and my notebook is crammed with such scintillating tidbits as "Eliza Dushku excited to be here" and "Dan DiDio claims 1) love of fan feedback, 2) no more dumb crossover events." I settle into my rental car and inhale a dense block of granola and dried fruit purporting to be an "energy bar." I'm headed to the rarefied air of Beverly Hills, to the Four Seasons, to Jack Camden.

Though all con happenings are situated in Downtown L.A.'s cavernous convention center, the publicist has insisted we meet at one of the city's ritziest hotels, perhaps to reinforce the notion that Camden is actually a celebrity. I arrive in a fairly speedy thirty-five minutes and steal away to the plush bathroom, where I attempt to bunch my unwieldy mass of hair into something that resembles a bun. Said hair, the hair that is so much like

Glory Gilmore's, refuses to be tamed by razors, scissors, or the industrial-strength ponytail elastics I buy in bulk at Target. As it is set against ghostly pale skin and light blue eyes, I have occasionally been informed that I appear slightly vampiric, and should therefore wear more velvet and engage in goth-y role-playing games. I prefer to think I'm rockin' an Aeryn Sun kind of look.

I duck back out into the lobby and am immediately assaulted by a pin-thin tornado of elaborately teased red hair—otherwise known as Kirstie Knight, GinormoCon press rep extraordinaire.

"Jules!" she trills, enveloping me in a bone-crushing hug. "What's up, girlfriend? Are you having a total blast?"

"Yeah, Kirstie, everything is great," I say, wincing a little at her sing-songy cadences. Kirstie is the only person I know who refers to me as "Jules." She's convinced that we're destined to have a special bond, being a couple of "gals" on the male-dominated geek press circuit. She enforces this by any means necessary, non-nicknames and all.

"You ready to meet the dreamboat?" she beams. "I swear, honey, he is even *better-looking* in person."

"I'm sure," I say, smiling thinly.

As Kirstie whisks me up to Jack Camden's room, I activate the persona I think of as Schmoozer Julie, aka Schmuzie. Schmuzie loves to talk about the marine layer near the San Francisco Bay, the fact that she's been working for *Mammoth Media* for about four years now, and what a pain going through airport security is these days—who even wants to fly anymore? Schmuzie expresses astonishment over L.A. traffic and agrees that GinormoCon is bigger than ever! No, Schmuzie hasn't seen that particular film, but she's heard good things. While Schmuzie chats with Kirstie, I retreat to the back of my head and go over my interview questions. Most of what I've got is pretty standard—I'm not planning on pulling any Vincent D'Onofrio-style interrogation tactics on Camden. I mostly just want to get this over with.

Finally, the elevator dings, Schmuzie agrees that this is the best season of *Periodic Seven* yet, and Kirstie ushers me into a room decorated in such neutral shades the furniture almost blends into the walls. Jack Camden is sitting on a beige and taupe striped couch, coffee-colored hair flopping rakishly over his stupid forehead. He's wearing a ratty Doctor Strange t-shirt, pseudo-distressed three-hundred-dollar jeans, and blinding white sneakers that look like they were only recently liberated from their factory box. Oh, and of course, the gleaming smile that's launched a million vomit-worthy Mary Sue fanfics.

"Jack, this is Julie from *Mammoth Media*," says Kirstie. "She's a big fan of the show."

"Hi, Julie," he says, shaking my hand, grin still firmly in place. "Nice to meet you. Are you covering the con?"

"Yeah," I say, settling into a chair across from him. "It's, you know... fun."

"Well, I'll just leave you two to chat," chirps Kirstie.

The door clicks behind her and I push the red button on my tape recorder, glancing down at my notes.

"So how did you land this part?" I ask, leaning forward and cocking my head to one side, miming genuine interest. "I know they did a huge search for Travis..."

"I auditioned and it was just one of those things," he says, shrugging. "I guess it was meant to be or something." He flashes a bullshit smile to let me know that this concludes his extremely-well-thought-out response, thank you very much.

"Didn't you have to do a chemistry read with Claire?" I ask. "She mentioned something about that when I interviewed her last year."

"Oh, yeah," he says, eyes rolling upward to focus on the eggshell-hued ceiling. "We read together and I guess there was something there. But I thought Claire was pretty cool right off. We kind of bonded over being really into comic books when we were kids. Only she actually grew out of the hobby."

This is one of Camden's stock responses—he's one of those pretty people who always tries to claim he was "such a nerd" in high school. His face is geometrically perfect, a ridiculously chiseled composition of sharp cheekbones and deep blue eyes. I can't picture it having a passing acquaintance with the notion of pimples.

"Right," I say, struggling valiantly to keep the sarcasm out of my voice. "I remember you saying that in your Scifi.com interview. And your *Us Weekly* interview. And—"

"Didn't know you'd memorized so many of my interviews," he cuts in, raising an eyebrow.

"Well, you know. Research."

He gifts me with another smile, this one containing a hint of condescension. "I *have* talked about a lot of this stuff before," he says. "Isn't there something else you want to know? I'm gonna be playing some gigs with my band…"

Oh, brother. No, Jack Camden, I do not want to hear about your fucking fake "band" and how music is your real passion. And even though I told myself I was going to stick to softballs in the name of getting out of here as quickly as possible, I decide to give him a little of what he wants. Different questions? Fine. Let's call him on some of those geek cred claims.

"Okay, how about this?" I say. "Since you were such a big *nerd* growing up, what were some of your favorite comic books?"

"All the usual suspects, I guess," he says, settling back into the couch. "The Batmans and Supermans and X-Mens and such. But actually, what I really loved were some of the weirder ones, like good ol' Doctor Strange here." He gestures to his shirt. "The Silver Age *Secret Six* was a big favorite. And…look, I know this sounds cheesy as hell, but I really dug the *Periodic Seven* comic. I was one of the ten people who read it." He smiles his "that's it" smile yet again.

Okay, name-checking *Secret Six* was a nice touch, but Camden obviously doesn't know what he's playing with here.

"Reaaaallllllllllllllly?!" I say, as if this is the most fascinating thing I have ever heard. "What was your favorite storyline?"

"Travis' big identity crisis and turn to the dark side was pretty cool," he says. "I keep wishing they'd do something with that on the show, but —"

"They kind of can't," I interject. "I mean, show continuity has it that—"

"Travis is incapable of lying after being infected with Doctor Halogen's nano-virus—I know." He shakes his head bemusedly. "That whole plot twist completely contradicts a lot of Travis' characterization in the original book. And it means I'll never get to have a goatee onscreen."

"You should consider that a lucky break," I blurt out before I can stop myself. "I mean, the way John Christofferson used to draw said goatee... Travis looked like he had a dead rat pasted to his face."

"Stop," he says, his smile reaching his eyes for the first time. "You're ruining my childhood dreams of badass facial hair. I totally had the Evil Travis issue 9 pinup on my bedroom wall."

"I don't believe it," I say, feeling a smile pulling at the corners of my mouth. "Because if it's the same pinup I'm thinking of, he was also wearing that awful head-to-toe bodysuit that made him look like a giant condom."

"And you knew what a condom was at such a tender age?" he says, grinning away. "Very advanced."

He leans forward and rests his elbows on his knees, studying me thoughtfully. "Do you remember the arc they did with Glory Gilmore?" he asks. "There was a whole thing in issues 10 through 14 where she loses her powers and she has to cope with being...well, regular. I'd actually say *that* was my favorite storyline."

Wait...*what*?

He takes my silence as encouragement. "It was sort of a metaphor for being, I don't know, lost? This big, tough superhero, and all of a sudden she's..." He frowns, searching for the words.

"Just a girl," I murmur.

"Yeah. Just a girl."

"I..." I seem to have developed a temporary mental block that keeps me from forming actual words. "I mean...that's. That's *no one's* favorite storyline."

"Oh, I know." He smiles ruefully, running a hand through his hair. "Most people think of it as a pretty low point in the book's run—broody, self-indulgent. But I gotta say—I loved it."

My brain suddenly stops processing regular thought. Instead, it's stuck on an interminable loop, a squeaky hamster wheel containing a single thought: *so did I*. My crabby little self felt Glory's pain.

Camden's perched on the edge of his seat now, smiling expectantly. I suddenly feel like his ever-present teeth-gleam is about to blind me. "Um, so," I say quickly, fighting to keep my voice bland. "Why don't we talk about your band?"

His smile falters. Confusion flashes across his face as he slumps back into the overwhelming beige of the couch. "Sure," he says slowly. "So I used to play bass in high school…"

I nod mutely, silently freaking out over my suddenly discovered commonality with the world's lamest person.

Later, I attempt to recuperate from the bizarre, possibly disastrous interview by shutting my generic Holiday Inn hotel room's stiff, mud-colored drapes and flopping onto the bed.

What the fuck was *that*?

Could it be…could it be that Camden somehow knew about my love for that particular plotline and mentioned it to fuck with me? Maybe he found my blog?

Unlikely. I blog anonymously and in obscurity. Which, really, is how most people should do it.

My cell phone buzzes and I flip it open, scanning through my texts. One from the editor, one from Braidbeard about how the new *Iron Man* movie footage "suxxors," and one from Mitch.

already had whedon sighting. party 2nite?

Damn, I almost forgot. I almost let dumbass Camden distract me from my mission. I text back in the affirmative.

Mitch, Braidbeard, and I have plans to attend a con-related bash thrown by the folks who maintain A Gathering of Elements, the big fan message board for the *Periodic Seven* show (sadly, a lot of the assholes who post there don't seem to be aware that it was even based on a comic).

I snap my phone closed and dig the palms of my hands into my squeezed-shut eyes until I see amorphous blobs of green and blue. At least for tonight, I will banish this whole Jack Camden weirdness from my mind. I have to be on my game at this party. Ready. Alert. Prepared to finally reclaim what was taken from me so long ago.

The party is being held at the Holiday Inn bar, so I change into a short black t-shirt dress and some knee-high boots and head downstairs. A glamorous cardboard sign with the words PRIVATE PARTY! has been affixed to the bar's entrance, where a couple of volunteers are checking in lined-up attendees.

"Heya." Mitch grabs my arm, pulling me into line next to him.

"Watch it," I say, slapping his hand. "The boardies are gonna think I'm cutting."

"Not my problem. I require beer. The faster we get in, the faster that's happening."

"Lush."

"Whatever, Miss Teetotaler," he says, smiling indulgently. "We all know about your anti-drinking stance. It coincides perfectly with your no-dating stance. You are one crazy mofo."

I roll my eyes at him. "I date. Sometimes." (I don't.)

"No." He shakes his head. "In terms of frequency, the No Drinks, No Dates spiel is second only to the anti-Jack Camden spiel." He affects a snotty, high-pitched tone that I guess is supposed to sound like me. "No matter what, people will always reveal their inherent lameness. It's awkward and uncomfortable and a waste of my fucking time."

Okay, that does sound a little bit like me.

"Say 'cheese' folks! Or, you know, whatever the geek version of 'cheese' is!" A camera flashes, turning the world into a collection of bright-white smudge creatures.

"Layla Lee," I say, rubbing my traumatized eyeballs. "Please delete whatever you just did immediately."

The tall, slender smudge in front of us lowers her gigantor-lensed instrument of torture. "Bah!" she snorts. "You think I've gone digital? This is all film, baby."

"You're a purist," Mitch says admiringly.

"I'm something," Layla agrees, fishing around in her massive camera bag. As usual, she looks like she got dressed in the dark, her holey, pill-ravaged t-shirt topped off with a coffee-stained button-down. As usual, she pulls it off, managing to appear elegantly artsy rather than homeless.

Layla plucks a pencil from her bag's depths. "Lovely to see you both," she says. "And please remember to throw any and all freelance work my way, especially if it involves Wookiee family portraits." She winds her long black hair into a makeshift top-knot, securing it with the pencil.

"Pretty sure that was a one-time deal," I say.

"The budget's tight right now," says Mitch. "But I've got your number."

"You do indeed," she beams at him, then zeroes in on his t-shirt. "'I Think I Love My Wife'?" she reads poking at his chest. "You're a newlywed now?"

Mitch goes all red and shifts away from her pointy finger. "It's a movie," he says. "Chris Rock?"

"Who?" Layla's brow wrinkles.

"Not important," Mitch mumbles.

"Mitch prefers to clothe himself exclusively in swag," I say quickly, trying to cover the awkwardness that seems to be overtaking our conversation. I gesture to his shirt and *Firefly* baseball cap. "Why pay for wardrobe when you don't have to?"

Layla cocks her head, top-knot flopping sloppily to the side. "I can get behind that," she says, smiling serenely. "Anyway, duty calls, but I'll see y'all later." She gives us a little wave.

I watch her stride away, impossibly graceful despite her general unkemptness. As the line shuffles forward, I turn back to Mitch, who still looks like he's impersonating a beet. "Oh, brother," I say. "Ask her out, already."

He shakes his head. "She's always got the con rats after her."

"Yeah, and most of 'em are hardcore Asian fetishists who look at her and see all their dearest hentai fantasies coming true. You appreciate…you know, her *art*."

"We'd have nothing to talk about," he counters. "She doesn't own a TV."

Despite being part of our geek press brethren (and a fellow San Franciscan), Layla Lee has about zero interest in pop culture. She uses the cash she makes snapping endless rounds of Hayden Panettiere candids to fund her fine-art photography, a collection of stark black-and-white images of gears and bolts and random bits of machinery. I normally find that sort of shit pretentious, but Layla's stuff is pretty amazing.

"So?" I shrug. "You can give her a fucking crash course in X-Men continuity and then she can take a bunch of pictures that symbolize your rageful feelings about Beast's secondary mutation."

He cocks an eyebrow. "Such romantic visions, coming from No Drinks, No Dates Girl."

"I have no objections to either of those things. As long as they're happening to other people."

"Hey there, kids!" As we reach the front of the check-in line, Barb, aka Camdenfemme57, gives us an expansive wave. Barb is one of the board's mods, a matronly, middle-aged woman who's never met a muted floral print she didn't like. Despite her rather mild exterior, Barb is mostly known in the *Periodic Seven* community for her extremely pornographic fanfic, most of which features Travis Trent paired with the team's other male members. "Great to see ya," she says, handing us a pair of "Hello, My Name Is…" stickers.

"Hi, Barb," Mitch says, slapping the sticker onto his tee. "I meant to tell you, I really enjoyed the latest chapter of *Forbidden Passion*."

"Mmmm," she beams. "Well, the dark deliciousness that is Travis-Gregory—or as I like to call it, Traegory—had to be explored further."

"I so agree," says Mitch, nodding solemnly. "And Julie loved it even more than me. If that's possible."

"Oooooooooh?" Barb trains her slightly manic gaze on me.

"Um, yes," I say. "You described all those positions very, uh… detailedly."

"That was my aim!" she squeaks. "I've been trying to finish the next chapter, but it's gonna have to wait 'til the kids are back in school."

"Looking forward to it," I lie as Mitch and I elbow our way into the party.

We both spot Braidbeard manning a table in the back of the room, thumbs and eyes surgically attached to his iPhone. "Okay," says Mitch, his gaze drifting to the bar. "Gallons of beer for me and a Coke for you. Meet you over at B's table?"

"Yeah, sure," I say, scanning the room distractedly. "Do you see the, uh…auction list?"

What, that memorabilia thing they're doing for charity? Isn't it all crap, like the glass Claire drank out of in episode forty-seven or whatever?"

"There's actually something I'm interested in," I say, keeping my tone ultra-casual.

"I think they have it back at the check-in table," he says. "I'm gonna get the drinks, but you knock yourself out."

I scurry back over to the check-in table, stealthily avoiding another Barb encounter, then oh-so-nonchalantly examine the clipboard containing the list. Most of it is, indeed, crap. But situated between an autographed cast poster and a lunch date with one of the show's PAs is what I'm after.

GLORY GILMORE ACTION FIG., ca.1989. MOC.

Come back to me.

She's listed seventh, so I've got a while to wait.

I arrive at Braidbeard's table just as Mitch is setting down our drinks.

"So," says Braidbeard, not looking up from his iPhone. "How was the big interview?"

"Oh, yeah!" Mitch grins. "Was Jack Camden the unapologetic dick you were expecting him to be?"

"Ya know, I really don't want to talk about it."

"Whatevs," smarms Braidbeard. "But you might want to know: there are *rumors* that a few cast members might be showing up here tonight."

"What?!" I say. "This is a fan party. Why would they come here?"

"Just what I *heard*."

"Hey, the auction is starting," says Mitch, nodding toward the front. "You ready to get your glass, Julie?"

"It's not the glass I'm after," I say lightly, drumming my fingertips on the tabletop. The caffeine is making me all jittery. Goddammit. This is why I don't drink. My system is way too delicate.

Still, I have to keep myself occupied until Item Seven comes up. Somehow, I manage to down three more Cokes.

And suddenly, time has passed with lightning speed and there she is, up front, her painted form as garish as ever. A tuxedo-clad volunteer holds her aloft. "This is a Glory Gilmore action figure from THE ORIGINAL COMIC BOOK," bellows Mr. Tux. "She is mint-on-card, folks—MINT-ON-CARD. Starting bid, please?"

Okay, I don't want to be the starting bid. The starting bidder always looks too desperate, and therefore usually ends up a loser.

"A dollar!" someone yells out, and everyone laughs.

"Come, now!" admonishes Mr. Tux. "Did I mention the MINT-ON-CARD part?!"

"Ten dollars!" comes a voice from the back.

Time to enter the fray.

"Twenty dollars!" I yell, pointing into the air as if I am giving a particularly rousing speech.

"Thirty!"

Uh-oh. Better go big.

"Fifty!" That should shut 'em up.

"Sevenny-figh!" someone slurs drunkenly.

I gulp. I gotta do it.

"One hundred dollars!" I scream.

That's not that much for getting back a piece of my soul, right? I can eat ramen for a couple weeks.

Silence. Crickets. I won! I won! I am triumphant! Take that, you motherfuckin' *Periodic Seven* comic haters! Take, that Mr. Tux! I showed you! I sho—

"One-fifty."

The voice comes from the back, cool and modulated. Kinda smirky-sounding. Kinda...douche-y. Oh, no. It can't be. I turn around as if in slow motion, imagining the Bionic Woman sound effect accompanying me all the way.

It is. It's…

"Jack Camden," breathes Braidbeard.

In the geometrically perfect, three-hundred-dollar-jeans-wearing flesh.

Another round of silence. What do I do? *What do I do?* Glory Gilmore is slipping away from me. Again.

"One-seventy-five!"

The crowd gasps. I gasp. Mostly because the person who just said that is…

"Braidbeard," I hiss. "What are you doing?!"

He looks at me very seriously, his mouth set in a firm line. Even his scruffy braids look solemn. "We're winning this," he says.

"Two hundred."

"TWO-FIFTY!" Now Mitch is getting in on it. "Julie," he says urgently. "We're gonna get this for you. We know how much you love bioempathy… Jack Camden can't possibly love it as much as you do."

"Frakkin' right!!!" yells Braidbeard.

"Biokinesis," I mutter.

"Three hundred." Camden. Of fucking course. He's located us in the crowd and is looking our way to see if we'll challenge that. I can't tell if he recognizes me or not, but there's something unpleasantly smug in his expression.

"Three…uh, twelve," says Braidbeard, suddenly looking a tiny bit unsure.

"Three-thirty!" says Mitch, even though he doesn't actually have to top Braidbeard's bid for us to win.

"Five hundred dollars."

"Argh!" cries Mitch.

"FRAKKIN'-FRAK!" screams Braidbeard.

"Buh," I say.

We are defeated.

"I need a refill." I dump the rest of my vodka tonic down my throat and slam the glass on the bar. Warmth burns through my belly as I gesture to the bartender, tapping the empty glass with my index finger. "Re. Fill."

"Maybe you wanna slow down a little." Mitch slides the glass out of my reach.

"Noooooo." I roll my head to the side, frowning at him. "I don...don't care about my delicate system. I care about *vodka*."

"It sucks that we didn't win," Mitch says carefully. "But you don't need to go off the deep end, here."

"You're...the deep end," I mumble as the bartender sets another icy glass in front of me. I cradle it in protectively to my chest.

"Let the woman drink, Mitchell," snarks Braidbeard, raising his own beverage—a fruity, umbrella-laden concoction—in salute. "She just suffered a crushing loss at the hands of the enemy."

Mitch rolls his eyes. "We'll get you another Glory Gilmore," he says, as if trying to soothe a recalcitrant child. "I promise."

"Shouldn't be too tough," says Braidbeard. "Especially considering that she's probably the least sought-after action figure this side of Jar Jar Binks."

"Shaddup," I growl.

"Hey, I am *in solidarity* here with you," declares Braidbeard, gesturing wildly with his glass. Foamy pink liquid sloshes over the side. "I'm all, like, giving rousing, season eight *Buffy*-style speeches and shit."

"God." Mitch buries his face in his hands. "How did I end up babysitting two of the most inexperienced drunks on the planet?"

"And Glory *is so* hard to find," I say, as if neither of them has spoken. I shake my head vehemently. "Nobody...nobody *likes* her. That's why she's hard to fin...find. This was my chance. And I *fucked it up*." I feel tears welling in my eyes.

"No, no...we frakked up *together*." Braidbeard plucks the umbrella from his drink and waves it back and forth like a teeny flag. "TEAM EFFORT FRAKKING UP. FOR THE WIN."

Mitch gives my shoulder a tentative squeeze. "Nobody fucked up," he says. "We were up against a TV star who makes more in an hour than most of us make in a year. Nothing to be ashamed of."

I stare at his giant freckled hand dwarfing my shoulder, blurring in and out of focus. "I know you think Glory's stupid," I say. "But I...she...when I was a kid..."

"I know." He reaches over and pries the vodka tonic out of my clenched fingers.

"She was different," I continue, my voice wobbly. "She didn't get along with...with *people*. Or maybe *people* didn't get along with her. When she lost her powers...she just wanted to be left alone. Why was that...is that... so hard for everyone to understand?" I scrape the back of my hand over my eyes.

"I don't know," Mitch says gently. "But I think maybe you need to call it a night."

I'm about to protest, but we're distracted by some ear-piercing screams emanating from the other side of the room. I crane my neck. Camden's dumb band appears to be setting up onstage. He carefully props his newly acquired Glory Gilmore up against the speaker.

"Damn," snorts Braidbeard, tossing the mini-umbrella into his empty glass. "Look at that asshole. Parading around like he's Nathan frakking Fillion. Totally rubbing it in."

As Camden adjusts the mic, he toasts the crowd with an overflowing shot glass. He downs the shot and grins his doofy grin, waving to the crush of girls shrieking his name.

I narrow my eyes, snatch my drink back from Mitch, and take a swig. Heat blazes through my chest and my limbs suddenly feel like Jell-O. I clutch the edge of the bar to keep from falling over. "He *is* rubbing it in," I hiss. "With his stupid...jeans and his...douchebag...*baggery*."

Camden plunks the shot glass down on the speaker, then turns and stumbles over an errant cable.

"By the looks of it, I think he's just enjoying the...spirits as much as you are," says Mitch, raising an eyebrow. He tugs on my arm. "Come on, let's go."

"Yeah, this party's dead anyway," Braidbeard staggers to his feet, then sits down quickly. "Um, gimme a second."

"I'm staying," I say, eyes glued to the Camdenized staged.

"Julie..." Mitch frowns.

"Stay. Ing." I take a healthy gulp of my drink. "And I think I wan... *want* to be alone right now, too. Ligglory."

"Like what?"

"Glooooaaaaarrrrrry."

He raises his hands in surrender. "Alright. Come on, B." Mitch helps Braidbeard to his feet, then leans over and grabs the bartender's arm. "Watch her, please? She just has to make it back upstairs, but I'd prefer she did so in one piece."

I shakily raise my glass. "Yourra good friend, Mishhh."

I down vodka tonics 'til I feel like I'm underwater.

Things begin happening in Blur Time. I'm floating away, outside my body, watching Drunk Julie (I guess this would be Drulie, not to be confused with Schmuzie) experience the world.

I watch as Camden's band takes to the stage, much to the delight of the fans. As he wails away on a passable version of "Surrender," Drulie can't help but rock out a little. She kinda digs this shit. No accounting for taste, I guess.

I watch as Drulie slinks up to the edge of the stage, where Glory Gilmore is still propped against one of the speakers. Wait, what the fuck is she doing?

I watch as she reaches and reaches, as she liberates Glory from her perch, just as Curtis did all those years ago.

And then she runs like hell, away from the party, away from "Surrender," away, away, away.

I watch as Barb, Mr. Tux, and some lame-ass "security" people chase Drulie down and start yelling, threatening to banish her from their stupid message board FOREVER.

I watch as another figure arrives on the scene, an extremely blurry figure with floppy hair and razor-sharp cheekbones and blinding white sneakers. He's telling Barb to calm down, just chill, everything's okay. He seems nice.

I watch and I watch and then everything blurs into more floaty nothingness.

Ow. Ow. Fucking ow.

I crack one eye open. Pain. Light. Lots of light. Way too much goddamn light.

Also, insides not feeling so good. I roll over in bed and scramble for something, anything, some kind of vestibule. I throw up into what I think is a wastebasket. I wipe my mouth on the back of my hand and stare blearily at the unlucky container that has just received the contents of my stomach. Brown, plastic, Holiday Inn-emblazoned. Somehow, I have made it back to my room.

I sit up gingerly (ow) and slowly open my eyes all the way, trying to bring my surroundings into focus. The muddy drapes are slightly cracked, allowing the offending light into the room. It shines way too brightly, illuminating the blank TV screen, the tangle of sheets, the bolted-down nightstand.

And perched on said nightstand, nestled in the folds of a crumpled Doctor Strange t-shirt, is a still mint-on-card Glory Gilmore.

Oh fucking *shit*.

– PART II –
SECRET ORIGINS

Trek Rules, Trek Fools

March 17, 2009

I know a lot of people think the Prime Directive is made to be violated.

I can already hear you shouting in that fucking shouty geek way. "It's dramatically necessary!" you are saying. "Any *Trek* captain worth his or her salt will get on that shit immediately!"

I, on the other hand, have always maintained that the general concept of non-interference is a pretty good idea (probably could've got home a lot sooner if you hadn't dicked so many Delta Quadrant societies around, *Janeway*).

It is, in fact, even a good idea when applied to our deceptively simple twenty-first century one-on-one relationships. I mean, look: most humans are kind of assholes. Entangling yourself with your fellow man—or woman—means you will carelessly entrust others with vital information about yourself. Information they may not be ready for.

Or, even more likely, information they will use against you. Trust me: the first tiny, spiteful chance they get, your fellow human will fuck you over. And then where will you be? Suddenly, the Alien Society of You is locked in full-on civil war, damaged beyond repair.

Now don't get all armchair psychologisty on me. My Alien Society is getting on just fine, thanks. But it's because I learned my lesson pretty early on. It's because I studiously apply my own personal Prime Directive whenever possible.

It works. Maybe it could work for you, too. Ya hearin' me, Janeway?

—*Posted on GloryGilmoreLives.com*

July 18, 2009
Five minutes past puke 'o clock.

All I want is a normal pair of sunglasses. The Holiday Inn gift shop is awash with plenty of *non-normal* sunglasses, let me just tell you. Sunglasses with rhinestones, with retina-singeing neon lenses, with Dora the fucking Explorer prancing down the curve of the earpiece. I spin frantically through racks and racks until I finally locate a nondescript gray pair that just screams "mall security" (or maybe "Section 31," if I'm lucky), pay for them, and stumble into the vicious daylight.

I stomp my way over to the convention center. Decisive footfalls. Energy expended. No room for thinking. No time to piece together certain images into...into...

Oh my fucking *God*. Frak. Frakking fuck. How could this—

No. Stop it. No thinking, only stomping! Brain is blank, blank, blank. These aren't the droids you're looking for.

I stomp through the heavy glass doors, past a trio of scruffy Darth Mauls, up and down the maze of corridors, finally arriving at my destination.

The GinormoCon autograph room is a sprawling expanse clogged with semi-orderly lines of people, all craving one tiny moment with their stalkee of choice. Jack Camden is settled into the far right corner, wearing a swag tee from last night's party and servicing a disgustingly long line of girls sporting clunky glasses and backpacks shaped like goggle-eyed anime characters.

I stomp my way through the lines, ignoring the barriers that have been set up to keep the various groupings of fankids separated from one another. A security minion waves his arms at me. "Miss...MISS! YOU CAN'T DO THAT!"

Well, normally I wouldn't, Sir Minion. I do have a decent amount of respect for nerd decorum, after all. But these are special circumstances. These are...these are...*cataclysmic* circumstances. *Final Crisis*-style, okay? Okay?! So in this case...yes, I fucking can.

After shoving aside a posse of Tyler Mane enthusiasts, I arrive at Camden's table. He doesn't notice me at first, so consumed is he by Sharpie-ing "XOXO" for the kazillionth time.

"Kaylee—what a cool name," he says, smiling winningly at the panda-ears-wearing girl in front of him. "Like on *Firefly*?"

"YES OH EM GEE YES!" she squeals, clapping her hands together. "YOU ARE MADE OF WIN!"

I clear my throat, glowering at Camden from behind my Section 31 shades. He finally looks up. Those brilliant blue eyes are kind of bloodshot today.

"Oh...um...hi," he stammers.

He glances at his adoring public, then back at me. "Listen, guys," he says, raising his voice to address the line, "I need a quick break. I'll be right back and then I'll sign everything. Promise."

He hops up from behind the table, places a hand firmly at the small of the back, and propels me through the crowd, out the door, across the hall. We land in an empty meeting room with a haphazard arrangement of tables and chairs and a buffet of sad-looking bagels.

"So," he says, stuffing his hands in his pockets and shifting uncomfortably. He can't seem to think of what comes after that. He tries to meet my sunglasses-obscured eyes. "You look, uh...pretty today."

Oh, Jesus. Does that line work on the clunky-glasses girls? Did it work on *me* last night?

"You got my note?" he asks.

"Yes," I say, trying to sound cool and formal. "Thanks for telling me where you'd be."

We share an awkward pause, our conversational skills apparently exhausted.

"Look," I say, snarling a little just to keep my voice from shaking. "Last night was a serious lapse in judgment for me. But I really need to know if you, uh…remember anything. Besides the sex."

Just saying it makes me a little nauseous. I slump into a chair next to the bagel buffet.

He just stares at me for a minute, his expression an almost comical mix of shock and confusion.

"Well…" He considers my query, pulling up a chair next to me. "We did use protec—"

"That's not what I mean!" I shriek. I feel like I might throw up. Again. "I mean. I remember the, um, making out and I remember the…other stuff. But I don't remember how we got all…you know. And I don't know what could possibly make me…" I stop myself abruptly.

But he gets it. Immediately. A bemused hint of smile plays across his face. "What could make you…get it on with a shallow, undeservedly famous guy with a vanity rock band?" he asks, sounding out each word carefully.

Argh.

"Yes," I say through gritted teeth.

"Huh." He leans back in his chair, trying—and failing fucking miserably—to keep the grin from spreading across his face. "Well, given that charming attitude of yours, I guess there's no question as to how I possibly could have resisted *you*."

I cross my arms over my chest, simmering.

"In all seriousness…we were both pretty lit," he continues. "You don't think we just got carried away?"

"I don't know," I say. "Maybe. But I just…feel like there was more to it than that."

Here's what I don't say: the moment I remember best, the image that is crystal-clear amidst the blurry mess of drunken debauchery, consists of five bizarre seconds wherein I sank my fingernails into the back of Jack Camden's neck and pulled him close, crushing his mouth with mine. I kissed him first. And I don't know why.

He's still trying to meet my gaze through my UV-blocking barriers. Finally, he lets out an irritated sigh and in one swift, decisive motion, reaches over and snatches my sunglasses, exposing my poor eyeballs to way more light than they're ready for.

"*Hey!*" I squint instinctively. Everything is too big, bright, blurry. "Give those back!" I yelp, batting ineffectually at the Camden-shaped blur.

He stuffs them in his pocket and looks me straight in the eye. "I *might* recall a few sordid details," he says.

"Okay," I say, squirming a little under the directness of his gaze. I manage to crack one eye all the way open.

"And I'd be happy to share, but I need to finish this autograph thing. So tell ya what—I have to put on an appearance at that *Level Up* party tonight. And I'm betting you have to do some kind of snarky write-up for your magazine. Right?"

"Yeah..."

"Okay. So let's have dinner beforehand."

"Like a *date*?" I huff. "No. No way. What happened last night is never fucking happening again. Ever."

"Hey!" he levels me with an exasperated look. "Not like that. We'll just get sandwiches from that disgusting snack machine in the cafeteria. I'll try to fill in some missing details and you will hopefully talk to me like a normal person instead of a profanity-spewing rageball. Okay?"

"I...okay." I glare at him so he knows this still does not please me at all.

"Okay." He reaches into his pocket and frees my sunglasses, passing them back to me. "7 p.m." He takes a few steps towards the autograph room and the gaggle of signature-hungry fangirls, then hesitates.

"Julie," he says, "do you remember what you said to me? When we got back to your room last night?"

"I told you," I say wearily, "I don't remember anything from the... between part. Why? What did I say?"

He hesitates, a touch of uncertainty creeping into his expression. "Never mind."

I find Mitch and Braidbeard in the food court, eating a dubious-looking breakfast of off-brand Cheetos and M&Ms. My sunglasses are back in their rightful place and I haven't even made a passing attempt at taming my hair, which is sprouting from my head like a pissed-off mushroom cloud.

"Well, well, *well*," says Braidbeard, taking in my disheveled appearance. "If it isn't the female Tony Stark."

"Goddammit, Braidbeard," I mutter, plopping into the seat next to Mitch. "That's so unoriginal. Can you at least find a female alcoholic to compare me to?"

"Like *who*?" he asks condescendingly. "The Tony Stark reference is a classic. It cuts across gender lines."

"What about Starbuck?"

"Sorry, but the only Starbuck *I* know of is a *man*—"

"Alright, you two," Mitch cuts in. "Nice to see that last night's drunken bond wasn't built to last. For twenty-four hours, even."

Braidbeard shrugs. "At least *I* know my limit."

Mitch turns back to me. "Julie, are you okay? We went up to your room last night to check on you, but there were…noises…"

"SEX NOISES," Braidbeard clarifies, apparently for the benefit of the three Klingons at the next table.

"Shhhhht!" I shush Braidbeard as Kang, Kor, and Koloth look on, probably wondering if my raging promiscuity extends to bat'leth-related Kama Sutra positions.

"I sort of…slept with someone," I say, hunching my shoulders and sliding down in my seat. Suddenly, I'm on the other end of a pair of uncomprehending stares.

In this moment, I realize that I better just tell them. Otherwise, I'm in for several rounds of increasingly uncomfortable questions.

I take a deep breath. "I slept with—"

"There's my favorite journalist!"

Oh, shit.

"Jules!" Kirstie whirls into view, pulling up a chair. "Girlfriend, you have some *explaining* to do!"

My hungover head throbs. "Um…"

"Nice to see you boys," she says to Mitch and Braidbeard, gifting them with a perfunctory nod. "So," she continues, spinning her tower of hair back toward me, "I heard you made a special friend at the Gathering of Elements soiree last night."

"What's that?" I croak. "Were you there?"

"Nooo, sweetie, I had, like, three other parties!" she giggles. "You know how crazy I am during the con. But a very reliable source told me that you were getting pretty chummy with that delicious Travis Trent!"

Fucking shit.

"I did...see him," I hedge.

"Mmmm-hmmm!" She gives me a knowing smile. "And to think...I introduced the two of you!" She claps her hands together, clearly delighted. "I gotta go check everyone in for roundtables, but you'll have to tell me every little thing later, Jules! See y'all around!"

With that, she spins her way out of view. And I am once again facing four perplexed eyeballs. I feel like a solitary french fry under the McDonald's heating lamp.

"Whoa," says Braidbeard.

"So," says Mitch, "this...person you slept with..."

"YOU DID IT WITH JACK CAMDEN!!!" yelps Braidbeard.

Those damn Klingons are really going to have something to talk about when they get back to Qo'noS.

"Yes, yes, okay, fuck!" I say, flopping forward so that my poor head hits the table. I decide to stay there for a moment. The plasticized tabletop is cool and soothing.

"Wow," says Mitch. "That's gotta be one of the most impressive con hook-ups of all time."

"Way better than anything from the pon-farr-themed room party at Shore Leave '07," agrees Braidbeard.

"And double points for frakking with the enemy," says Mitch. "Was it hotter than Barb's last fanfic?"

"Very fucking funny," I say, my head still resting on the table. My mushroom cloud of hair has fallen over my eyes, obscuring my vision, enclosing me in a black hole.

Still, I can practically feel Braidbeard smirking.

"Weelllllll, peeps," he says, drawing out each syllable, "I could chat all day about how Julie's little indiscretion is a continuity-frakking twist on par with organic webshooters, but I gotta prep for my Graham Barrett interview."

"Eh?" I say from under my hair, suddenly interested in something beyond my own suffering. "How'd you get that? I thought he wasn't doing any press—you know, as usual."

"He made an exception for *me*," gloats Braidbeard. "I guess he's a fan of my column."

"The site, B," says Mitch mildly. "He's a fan of the *site*. At least according to his people, and they're probably lying. They know he needs some decent PR if he expects to make the leap from superstar comics writer to Hollywood hack. That cranky British 'I don't give a shit about the fanboys who made me famous' mystique is only gonna get him so far."

"Well, whatevs," sniffs Braidbeard. "I gotta go. Have fun being jealous. Oh, and try not to sleep with anyone today, Julie."

Without raising my head, I lift a middle finger at his departing back.

"Okay," says Mitch, once we're alone, "I know you didn't want to get into it too much in front of B, but I really am curious. You getting your inner con slut on is an event to begin with. But you getting your inner con slut on with Jack Camden is like...I don't know, the oh-em-gee time leap in *Battlestar Galactica*. I need more details."

I shove my hair out of eyes, push my sunglasses on top of my head and glare at him.

"Ya know," he says, ignoring my death-ray stare, "I wouldn't think less of you if you, like, *enjoyed* it."

I groan. "Why are you being so nosey?"

He shrugs, wiping his Cheeto-dusted fingertips with a napkin. "I tell you shit, don't I? I mean, what about my awesome...encounter with that *Ghost in the Shell* girl at WonderCon? You loved that one."

I did love that one.

"I would ask you to tell it again right now if my head didn't hurt so much," I say. "If only for the part where you found out what she was using to keep all of her, um, access points in place."

"Right," he says, smiling fondly at the memory.

I lower my sunglasses back over my eyes. "While we're on the subject," I say, "Layla Lee probably has some decent...access points."

"That has nothing to do with anything," he says dismissively. He nudges me in the shoulder. "Come on—spill. Were there...fireworks?"

I heave a mighty sigh. "It was...fine."

But as I say this, a few choice images flash through my mind. A few choice images that involve Jack Camden being pretty naked. It must be said that they are way better than "fine."

Now I'm *really* going to throw up.

After a nap and half a bottle of Advil, I'm feeling reasonably human by the time night rolls around. As promised, Camden is waiting for me outside the tiny cafeteria at 7 on the dot. This time, he's added something new to his comics-themed tee/luxury-brand jeans ensemble.

"Glasses?" I say, taking in the Rupert Giles-esque wire-rimmed specs perched on his nose. "Are you trying to blend in with us nerds?"

"I am one of you nerds," he says, smiling wearily. "And my contacts were killing my eyes."

"I brought you your shirt," I say, thrusting a wadded gray blob in his direction. He accepts it, balling it up in one hand. "And your, uh...Glory Gilmore." I lift the flap of my messenger bag to show him Glory, still safe in her packaging. He studies her for a moment, his eyes unreadable.

"I think...I think she's yours now," he says.

"Uh, okay. Whatever."

We proceed to the cafeteria, a cramped, marginally functional box done up in blah institutional grays and strewn with yesterday's newspaper and wrinkled GinormoCon fliers. The food court is closed for the day, so the only option for con-goers in need of sustenance is the oddball assortment of vending machines bunched into a corner of the room. We seem to be the only ones opting for this gourmet adventure tonight.

Camden fishes a handful of change from his pocket. The biggest vending machine is the kind that rotates through its selection with a touch of a button, offering your choice of mummified, plastic-encased sandwiches for two bucks a pop.

"So what'll it be?" he asks, pressing the button and watching the sandwiches spin in and out of view. "Ham? Egg salad? What kind of food poisoning do you want?"

"Um, I'll get my own," I say.

He raises an eyebrow. "I promise this still isn't a date," he says. "But I can buy you a sandwich."

"Okay, okay," I relent. "Ham. Egg salad is just asking for it."

He pulls our sandwiches free from the case and we sit. The vending machines chorus together in a low hum as we unwrap our dinner.

"So," I say, twisting the plastic wrap between my fingers, "will you... tell me what you remember?"

He looks at me thoughtfully, as if he's trying to recall the exact details of my face (probably, he is—surely I'm one of many con-quests). I almost expect him to launch into some sort of game-playing, to flash a pseudo-suave grin and ask me how much *I* remember. Instead, he considers for a moment, then answers.

"Well," he says hesitantly, "as I recall—and I swear I'm not saying this to bullshit you—you made the first move."

I nod quickly, my cheeks flaming. This is the problem with being vampire pale—you can't exactly hide it when you're totally fucking embarrassed.

"But right before you, um, kissed me, you sort of...leaned in, like right next to my ear. And told me stuff."

"*Stuff?*"

"About Glory Gilmore and how some douchebag stole your action figure in college and how it was really important for you to get it back. And—" He stops abruptly, raking a hand through his floppy hair. Maybe it's just the unnatural fluorescent glow of the vending machines, but I'd swear he's starting to flush a little bit.

"And...what?"

He is suddenly extremely interested in dissecting his sandwich, lifting the top slice of bread and gingerly picking off a paper-thin piece of tomato. He replaces the bread and takes a bite, his eyes focusing on a point just above my right ear.

"That's it."

"Oh, really?"

"Yup. Hey, this sandwich isn't so bad."

"Huh," I say, sitting back in my chair and folding my arms over my chest. "Well, thanks for sharing. It must be really hard to remember all these details, considering the parade of fangirls you've already slept with this weekend. Think you'll pull a Jimmy Doohan and marry one?"

He chokes a little on his bite of sandwich. "Whoa," he says. "So that cloaking device of hostility you've got going on wasn't just for our interview, huh?"

I shrug.

"Okay," he says, putting the sandwich down and meeting my gaze. "First of all, no fair using the dead for your sarcasm. Second, you're the only fangirl—the only *person*—who I've had the, uh, pleasure of bedding at a convention. And third...maybe you want to summon the incredible reserve of energy you've got powering that Emma Frost-worthy 'tude and use it to remove the gigantic chip from your shoulder. I don't have to be doing this, you know. Talking to you."

"Then why are you here?" I say, setting my glare to maximum.

"Because..." he looks at me consideringly, propping an elbow on the table and resting his chin on his palm. "Because you asked. Do you remember that? *You* asked. You wanted to solve this big drunken mystery, Girl Detective."

He locks his eyes on mine and I shift uncomfortably. I feel like he can see right through my skull, into my freaked-out little brain. Must be pretty fucking entertaining.

"I...dammit," I mutter. I tear my gaze away from his, my eyes wandering to my untouched sandwich. I poke a hole in the squishy white bread. My arsenal of acidic retorts evaporates from the tip of my tongue, floats off into the fluorescent-lit air. And all of a sudden, a bunch of *other* words are spilling out before I can stop them. "This is...just. I don't have a lot of…experience," I say awkwardly. "I mean, with this sort of thing. I don't usually drink. Or steal. Or…do what we did. And I really wish I could remember more. And I met Jimmy Doohan once and he was really nice. He even took a picture with me."

He nods, encouraging me to keep up my stream of LiveJournal-y babble. I'm not really recognizing this yammering girl who won't shut the hell up. Maybe she's Bizarro Schmuzie?

"I…" I swallow hard. "The idea that I completely lost all control, especially with…"

He raises an eyebrow.

"…with…uh, someone I just *interviewed*," I say quickly, shutting down the rogue LiveJournaler before she gets totally out of hand. "I mean, it's pretty fucking unprofessional, to say the very least."

He lets that hang for a moment. "Wow," he finally says, grinning a little. "That actually sounded sort of like something a human would say."

"Hey!" I reinstate my glare. "You know, it's not like you came off very well in our interview, either. Could you maybe come up with a few one-liners that aren't already part of your Wikipedia entry?"

He looks surprised, then slouches back in his chair. "I hate interviews."

"Really? Talking about yourself isn't high on the 'awesome' list?"

He shakes his head vehemently. "No. It's…embarrassing."

"You didn't seem embarrassed. You seemed in pretty full-on fakey TV-star mode, actually."

"Yeah, well. It's basically just another kind of acting," he says. "You put on this front to get through it, or you'll come off like an asshole. Memorized sound bites are your friends."

I raise an eyebrow. "And the chatting up of the fangirls? The 'Oh, *Kaylee*, tell me more about your panda ears and the name you're probably misspelling on purpose in order to appear more Whedon-esque?' What's *that*?"

He crumples his sandwich wrapper into a tiny ball, balancing it on top of the abandoned tomato. "It's…being what they want me to be." He shrugs, giving me a rueful smile, a very distant cousin to the Jack Camden megawatt grin. There seem to be fewer teeth involved. "Another kind of cloaking device."

I tilt my head, studying him as he rolls the sandwich wrapper ball to the end of the table and catches it in his other hand. He has nice hands. Or at least, they felt nice when they were running up and down my bare—

JESUS. What the hell is wrong with me? Put it back in your pants, LiveJulie.

I force my eyes back up to his face. "Are you trying to tell me you're *shy*?" I can't keep the skepticism out of my voice.

"Not so much that as…socially weird." He tips his head to the side, and looks at me thoughtfully, his forehead crinkling. "But I do have the ability to manufacture schmooze."

I cock an eyebrow. "So the getting up on stage and pretending you're a rock star? That helps you get your tragic TV heartthrob angst out?"

He smiles crookedly. "Something like that. I also just, you know…enjoy playing bass."

"But why the nerd act, then? Where does that fit in?"

"Man." He shakes his head at me. "Julie. What do I have to do to get you to believe I am one of your people?"

"I just—"

"Wait." He suddenly sits up very straight, his eyes glazing over in a way that might charitably be referred to as "slightly demented." He turns this disconcerting gaze on me. "I know."

He stands up abruptly, sweeping the remnants of his sandwich into the trash. Then he grabs my hand, pulling me to my feet, and drags me toward the door. He's a possibly crazy man on a mission, his face set in a mask of grim determination. Maybe it's the full-on weirdness of the whole situation, but I don't even blink when he says, in the single worst Schwarzenegger impression I have ever heard, "Come with me if you want to live."

We end up not in some Skynet-plagued future, but at the party we were both supposed to attend in the first place. With the help of a few prominently placed corporate sponsors (whoo, Red Bull!), the folks at *Level Up*, a long-running gamers' magazine, have taken over one of the con center's ballrooms, turning it into a blaring whirlwind of gaming stations and alcohol (which I will be steering clear of tonight, thank you very much).

"What are we—"

"Shhh!" Camden shushes me as we approach the check-in table, which Kirstie is presiding over with great verve.

"Oh, my!" she chirps, her face lighting up like the TARDIS. "I guess the party can *really* start now!"

"Hi there, Kirstie," says Camden. "I think I'm on the VIP list?"

"Of course, darling," she says. "And Jules, you're on my press list." She cups her hand next to her mouth, exaggerating the gesture as if she's about to share a particularly juicy secret. "Jack, watch out for *this one*!" she stage-whispers. "She's a wild gal!"

"I believe it," he says, grinning. "Listen, I also wanted to sign up for the tournament. Can I still do that?"

"Yup," she says scribbling something on one of her complicated-looking grids. "You'll be an exciting last-minute addition. It starts in five."

"Great, thank you."

I shoot Camden a quizzical look. "What are you…"

"You'll see. Come on."

We make our way into the dark, pulsating ballroom, which looks and sounds like the big rave in the lamest of the *Matrix* movies, only everyone's wearing baggy, logo-emblazoned t-shirts instead of neutral-colored sacks made out of hemp. The only flickers of light are emanating from the various TV screens set up around the room, housing images of death, destruction, and really awesome cars.

"Julie! Hey!" Mitch and Layla Lee approach us, Mitch raising a beer, Layla fiddling with her ever-present camera. Apparently, a gaming party is an officially fancy event, as Mitch has broken out his favorite piece of wearable swag: the much-coveted *Hot Fuzz* t-shirt, which features an intense-looking silkscreen of Pegg and Frost, plus the ominous words

"This Shirt Just Got Real." Layla, meanwhile, is wearing something that looks like a cross between a grocery bag and a pillowcase.

"Hey, Mitch," I say. "Layla." I look from one to the other, taking note of their togetherness, and raise an eyebrow in Mitch's direction. He gives me a look that says Don't Start.

"Hey," says Camden, reaching out to shake Mitch's hand. "Jack. We've talked before, right? The season two junket, was it?"

"Yeah," says Mitch, looking moderately starstruck.

"Nice to see you again," says Camden. "Cool shirt."

"Thanks," Mitch says faintly, blushing a little. Great. In addition to his predilection for girls dressed as cyborgs, it looks like he also has a bit of a Camden man-crush. "Oh, and this is Layla."

Layla shakes Camden's hand, shooting me a decidedly unsubtle "OhmyGAWD" look. I realize that, being Layla, she probably doesn't know who he is. She just thinks that after years of con celibacy, I've managed to bag myself a hottie.

"Can you believe this frakkin' thing?" Braidbeard saunters up to us, his nasal intonations cutting through the party's frenetic bleeps and bloops. "Hey, man," he adds, nodding oh-so-casually in Camden's direction.

Suddenly, a spotlight overtakes the center of the room. I squint in its general direction. A mammoth TV screen sits atop a makeshift stage, a tiny, tuxedo-clad figure standing directly in front of it. Actually, I think it's Mr. Tux from the auction the night before. Maybe he's the only convention guest who owns formalwear.

"Ladies and gents!" he bellows. "Welcome, welcome, welcome to the *Level Up*-Red Bull-Sony-Helio par-TAY, brought to you in part by MySpace! At this moment, we're going to start the highlight of the night...our first annual *GUITAR HERO* TOURNAMEEEEENT!"

Drunken cheering abounds.

"Okay," says Mr. Tux. "Here's how this is gonna work. We have ten... oops, make that eleven contestants! We'll have two brackets, with our players facing off song by song. The final two will advance to our last round, which features a super surprise TWIST! Got it?"

Another slurry round of cheering practically has the room vibrating. I turn to Camden, my eyebrow raised. "This? This is how you're going to show your true geek colors?"

He grins and shoves the balled-up Doctor Strange tee in my direction. "Hold this for me, will you?"

"Huh," I say. "But don't you know how to play the real guitar because of your band? Doesn't that give you an unfair advantage?"

He leans in close so I can hear him over the ruckus. "Julie," he says softly, "any true geek knows that actually playing guitar counts for nothing in *Guitar Hero*. If anything, it's a handicap."

I nod mechanically, but suddenly all I can focus on is his fingertips brushing my arm and how close his mouth is to my ear and a rather vivid flashback of that mouth drifting from ear to neck to…other places. A little shiver flashes through me and my entire face is suddenly blazing hot. I shift uncomfortably. Maybe I'm getting the flu.

"Okay!" screams Mr. Tux. "Let's bring forth our first challengers. May I please have Greg Roberts and Jack…Camden?" He squints at the card to make sure he's read it right. "Well!" he exclaims as Camden saunters toward the stage. "Looks like we have a CELEBRITY CONTESTANT! Ladies and gents, TV's very own Travis Trent is IN THE HOUSE!"

"Wow!" chirps Layla, snapping a quick series of shots. "He's famous, too? Major score, Julie."

Camden ascends the stage to wild cheers, shaking hands with the other contestant—a skinny guy in a long leather duster—and accepts his plastic guitar from Mr. Tux. He chooses a bright-haired punk chick as his avatar and stands at the ready while Leather Duster selects a shifty-looking dude with a freakishly large torso. They both gaze intently at the screen, fingers poised over the primary-colored plastic of their guitar controls, as the first song loads up.

I glance over at Braidbeard and Mitch. They're both completely riveted, eyes bugged wide, mouths slightly agape. "Aweeesooooooooome," breathes Braidbeard, practically singing out the word.

The song, "Barracuda," is a bit of a lightweight for the true *Guitar Hero* enthusiast—but on expert mode, it's still pretty fucking crazy.

For the first verse or so, Camden and Leather Duster are neck and neck, strumming the thumping pseudo-chords with precision, heads bopping along in near unison. Then Camden flubs a tricky run of notes, falling behind.

"Star power," murmurs Braidbeard. "He's gotta do it."

When the dusting of stars appears onscreen, I inhale sharply. But Camden knows exactly what to do, tilting his miniature axe into the air with greater-than-necessary flourish. Punky Girl lights up in response, emanating a supernatural glow, spinning her guitar around her leg. Leather Duster, unfortunately, is a little slower on the uptake. No dubious acrobatics for his avatar.

"ALRIGHT!" Braidbeard shrieks, pumping a fist in the air.

"You okay, Julie? You looked a little nervous there for a minute," says Mitch.

"I'm fine," I say. "It's just stuffy in here. Hard to breathe."

After that, Leather Duster never recovers and Camden strums his way to a fairly ass-kicking victory.

"Wow," says Mitch, lifting an eyebrow. "Your new boyfriend is pretty good."

"Not bad," I say, trying to appear unimpressed. "But that was one song and the Angel wannabe up there was pretty slow on the uptake. There's no way Camden can beat the nerd elite."

And yet, as the challengers come, he takes them down one by one. He bests a combat-booted goth girl on "Black Magic Woman," whips a stone-faced teenager at "Rock You Like a Hurricane," narrowly beats out a Harry Knowles doppelganger on "Raining Blood."

Meanwhile, Barney Springshorn, a gangly, fedora-sporting gamer who I recognize from his popular blog, cruises to victory in the other bracket. He and Camden are the last men standing. "ALRIGHT," bellows Mr. Tux. "These two fine gentlemen will move on to our very special FINAL ROUND. Now. I told you there was a surprise twist, didn't I?!"

The crowd screams in the affirmative.

"Right!" says Mr. Tux. "These gods of gaming will NOT be playing *Guitar Hero*!!!"

There's a collective gasp. "Fuckin' weak *sauce*!" someone yells.

"RATHER," continues Mr. Tux, undaunted, "they will have to prove their might in another milieu! We're gonna have them face off in an oldie but goodie, in that staple of arcades AROUND THE WORLD…"

"BOOOOOO!" screams the heckler.

"This dynamic duo will be demonstrating their best moves innnnnnnnn…*DANCE DANCE REVOLUTION!!!*"

The crowd actually doesn't know quite what to make of *that*.

"And," says Mr. Tux, rushing ahead to cover up the sudden silence, "here's another TWIST. Both gentlemen will need to find a PARTNER to compete with! It will be…a DOUBLE *DANCE DANCE* DUEEEEEL!"

The crowd, having had time to recover (or maybe just down another beer), finally gets it together and lets loose with an ear-splitting cheer.

"Come back in thirty minutes!" cries Mr. Tux. "And our champion will be REVEALED!"

With that, the pulsing music comes back over the loudspeaker and the room explodes into excited chatter. Camden steps down from the stage and wends his way through the mass of people, stopping here and there to receive the occasional high-five.

"Kick-*ass*, man!" exclaims Braidbeard, as Camden rejoins us.

"Really sweet," says Mitch, handing him a beer.

"Visually stunning," says Layla, snapping away.

They all look at me expectantly.

"That was…neat," I finally manage.

"Well," says Camden, "I suppose you've already cycled through expert mode on every song in existence, right?"

"HA!" Braidbeard snorts. "Julie is sooooo not a gamer. She's like the Meg White of *Guitar Hero*."

"Hey, come on now," says Mitch. "That's not really fair to Meg White."

"My geekdom lies in other areas," I sulk.

"Uh-huh," Camden looks at me bemusedly. "What areas would those be?"

"I don't know…everything else?"

"Comics, for sure," says Mitch.

"Ahhh, yes." Camden's expression softens. "I know that much." He meets my gaze for a moment, the flickering lights distorting his features in the dark.

Shiver, blush. Hot, cold. Fucking flu.

"Hey, let's...let's go hang in the hall," I stammer. "I really can't breathe in here."

"I've gotta stay," says Layla. She gestures to her camera. "Atmosphere shots."

The rest of us file out, Braidbeard keeping up a steady stream of questions about Camden's fake guitaring technique as we proceed to the less claustrophobic confines of the hall. "So in expert mode, do you think it's better to keep your index finger on the red or the green?" he asks, brow furrowed. "I've heard arguments for both, but I'm just not convinced green is a viable option..." I groan, tuning him out.

"So," says Camden, once we've made it to the cool, open space beyond the party. "What's with your non-gamer status? It's throwing me for a loop, here."

"I just can't get into any of it," I say. "It seems like such a time-suck. You spend hours and hours doing the same bullshit over and over and what do you get at the end? A fake princess? Bragging rights on some fucking message board? Pointless."

"Also," says Mitch, leaning into Camden conspiratorially, "she's really bad at them."

"I'm sure if I put in as much effort as you, Mitch, I too could easily become a level 5000 mage on *World of Warcraft*," I say. "But I just don't care."

"There is no level 5000," says Braidbeard. "Unless they added that in the new expansion pack—"

"I *know*," I say hotly. "I was exaggerating."

"Okay," says Camden. "But why are comics and TV and all that any better? Isn't there a time-suck element there, too?"

"There's storytelling," I say. "Relationships. Something for me to get really invested in that doesn't involve clicking on a certain configuration of buttons."

"Uh-huh," Camden nods, looking less than convinced. "You have a lot of theories about stuff, don't you?"

"Yeah, you should hear the one she has about yo—OW!" I deliver my best Vulcan nerve pinch before Braidbeard can get the rest of his sentence out. He shoots me a wounded look.

"Alright," says Camden, looking thoughtful. "So I know you're all about the Glory Gilmore. Who else?"

"Jean Grey," I say. "Jenny Sparks."

"The Spirit of the Twentieth Century," Camden intones theatrically, a hint of his crappy Schwarzenegger impression creeping in. "Jenny, I get. But Jean? I still think you've got more of an Emma thing going on. Speaking of which, what are your thoughts on the unholy union between Miss Frost and Scott Summers?"

"Oh, no," mutters Mitch.

"Fucking lame," I say. "Two great characters made un-great by a totally contrived relationship."

"And...?" Mitch eggs me on.

"And!" I say, pointy finger gesticulating all over the place. "We spent how much time believing in Jean and Scott? They go through this whole epic thing and there's death and reunion and pining and all of these struggles that aren't just, like, 'men are from Mars,' but are life and fucking *death*. They're this endgame couple, right? Then when they're actually together, what happens? Cyclops can't keep his psychic dick in his pants."

"Well," says Camden, as I try to catch my breath, "there was a little more to it than *that*. Sounds like you've got kind of a nostalgia death grip on the storylines you liked as a kid. This is all very fascinating, though—I didn't know you were such a romantic."

Before I can respond to this infuriating little morsel, we're interrupted by a svelte figure clad in a black tank top and ass-boosting jeans. She's teetering down the hall in her glittering high heels when she spots Camden and stops abruptly. "Jack?"

"Oh...hey, Claire." He goes a little pale, shifting awkwardly from foot to foot. I glance from him back to the high-heeled interloper and realize that I recognize her. Her hair is usually dyed jet-black when she's playing Glory Gilmore, but she's let it grow out now that *The Periodic Seven's* on summer hiatus. Her blondish-brown roots hug the top of her scalp, her tresses pulled back into a sleek ponytail. She's Claire Yardley, Camden's onscreen co-star. "What are you doing here, anyway?" he asks. "I wasn't expecting to see you 'til the panel tomorrow."

"I promised I'd do a little appearance at the party—and hey, open bar," she says, giggling and flicking her ponytail over her shoulder. "I saw you up there, putting your best...skills to use. Are you all set to bust a move?"

"I...I dunno," he says, eyes wandering to the floor and staying there.

"Oh, Jack," she pouts a little, but her eyes never lose their mocking spark. "What's wrong? You can't find anyone to dance with? I bet one of your little nerd-girl fans would be up for it. Of course, she'll probably bolt once she sees your doll collection."

"They're not dolls," he mutters peevishly. "They're die-cast robots from Japan and some of the older ones were really hard to find."

"Uh-huh." The right corner of her mouth curls into a humorless grin. "Well, maybe your mad eBay skills can also help you find, you know, *the one*."

He meets her gaze, eyes shrouded in hurt. "Why do you...just stop it," he says, his voice drifting to a whisper. He stuffs his hands in his pockets, shoulders hunched, lips pressed tightly together. His entire body is caving in on itself.

"Oh, babe, you know I'm just teasing," she says, rolling her eyes. "God. Anyway, I bet all the little gossip blogs would just love it if you had to forfeit. Why don't you give them something to talk about?"

"No." The voice is thin but determined. And inexplicably coming from my mouth. Aw, fuck. I think it's that stupid LiveJournal-y girl.

Mitch and Braidbeard, who have been watching in stunned silence as two of TV's biggest superheroes exchange these decidedly unheroic words, whip their heads in my direction. Claire raises a plucked-to-all-hell eyebrow, noticing me for the first time.

"He's not forfeiting," I say firmly. "I'm his partner—dance partner!" I awkwardly grab Camden's hand to enforce this notion. It seems like the thing to do. He looks at me vacantly.

"And," I continue, "some of those robot imports *are* hard to find. Especially at a decent price."

"Huh," she cocks her head to the side, her face a mask of condescension. "Well, like I said, Jack—you can always count on your *fans*. Good luck!" Before any of us can respond, she pivots on her spiky shoe and stalks off, ponytail swinging insolently.

We exhale in unison. I realize I'm still clutching Camden's hand in a death grip and drop it like a hot rock.

"I..." Camden's bewildered gaze flicks from me to Mitch to Braidbeard. "I'm sorry...about that. Excuse me." He hobbles a few feet away and sits down hard on the floor, leaning against the wall. He looks like Eeyore, post-tail loss. Like he can't get back what's been taken away, even though it's right there, within reach. Something in my gut twists, a long-dormant but familiar ache.

"Wow," breathes Braidbeard, shaking his head in awe. "Travis Trent. Pwned."

"Give me a sec," I murmur. I stride over and slide down the wall, sitting next to him.

"Hey," I say softly. "Thank you."

"For what?" His knees are drawn up in front of him, arms resting limply on top, hands balled into fists. He won't look at me.

"For giving me Glory Gilmore," I say. "That was really cool. Thank you."

He doesn't respond. I take a deep breath and try a different tack. "So," I say carefully. "Bad break-up?"

"Yeah," he says, eyes still glued to the floor. "I thought...I mean, I told her. That she was, um, the one. It may have involved a homemade card with a *Matrix* reference." I wince a little. "I couldn't see what she really was," he continues, shaking his head. "But while I was making my stupid card, she was banging the executive producer. And possibly his assistant. She said she didn't realize we were—" he goes into a fairly decent impression of Claire's bored cadences "—like, *serious*." He finally meets my eyes, mortification haunting his entire face. "That was a year ago. We're... we're okay on-set. She's professional, you know? Cordial. But whenever I have to see her in a social way, it just...fucks me up. Stupid." He sighs, flopping his head back against the wall with a dull "thunk."

We sit there for a moment in silence. Finally, he seems to come to a resolution. "Enough of this," he says. "I'm gonna go tell Barney he's officially the champion."

"*No.*" There's that damn voice again. I'm kind of starting to like her. Go on, LiveJulie. "Camd—Jack," I say. "I meant what I said. I'll be your partner."

He looks at me uncomprehendingly, glasses sliding down his nose.

"Look," I say, eyes narrowing. "Are you really gonna let that...that *Mundane* get to you?" I root around in my messenger bag, pulling out Glory Gilmore. I quickly and expertly liberate her from her packaging. The molded plastic makes a satisfying "pop" as it separates from the stiff cardstock. Camden looks slightly horrified—yet intrigued—by my blithe destruction of her mint-on-card-ness.

I brandish the newly freed Glory in front of his nose. "What would Glory Gilmore do?" I ask. "Not that fucking poser with the stupid shoes. The *real* Glory Gilmore. Remember in issue 17 when Doctor Halogen released his deadly airborne toxin into the city? It crippled the rest of the Seven?"

He nods slowly. "Glory was the only who wasn't affected—she was inside, in the lab. But she couldn't go help them, because she'd be exposed to the gas."

"Right." I nod approvingly. "So what did she do? Did she just sit around and whine and bitch and *take it*?"

"No," he whispers.

"That's fucking right!" I exclaim, waving plastic Glory around. "She used her mad scientist skills—her *human* skills, the ones she had before she became a superhero—to formulate an antidote. Then she kicked Doctor Halogen's *ass*."

I take Jack's hand, gently uncurling his balled-up fist, placing Glory in his open palm. I look him dead in the eye, enunciating each syllable.

"What...would...Glory...Gilmore...do?"

He smiles a little half-smile, coming to life at last. "Okay," he says. "Let's go."

As it turns out, Barney is a pretty good Dance Dancer. He's recruited a friend who looks like his even lankier clone and they're stomp-stomp-stomping away, following the merciless rain of onscreen arrows.

"This should be interesting," Jack says, watching them go. "What with you not really being a gamer and all."

"Are you actually objecting to my incredibly generous offer?" I say.

"No, no," he assures me. "I appreciate it. A lot."

Barney and BarneyClone finish off their routine with flair, landing in place on the dance pad. "ALRIGHT," yells Mr. Tux, as the audience cheers. "Very nice. Now, let's bring out finalist number two. Once again, I give you…JACK CAMDEN! And, er…PARTNER!"

Jack gives a little wave to the crowd as we stroll across the stage. I squint into the light, trying to pick out Mitch and Braidbeard and Layla, but all I see is a mass of misshapen, big-mouthed faces, like everybody's just watched that fucked-up video in *The Ring*. We take our places on the side-by-side dance pads and train our eyes on the screen.

The song boots up. It's a random Japanese jam that sounds like the opening theme for an aggressively-perky-bordering-on-frightening kids' TV show. I take a deep breath. Step, step…stepstepJUMPJUMPstomp stepstomp…

Jack tears his eyes from the screen for a split second, glancing in my direction. "WHAT…WHAT?!"

"EYES ON THE SCREEN, JACK!" I bark. Jumpstepstomp stompJUMP…

Okay. Here's the truth. I'm really fucking good at *Dance Dance Revolution*. It is the only game in the known 'verse that I am actually good at. I somehow ended up with *Mammoth Media's* free review copy and dance pad and hooked it up one night in a fit of insomnia-induced boredom. I may not be a level 5000 mage in some made-up world, but I can do expert mode on "In the Navy." Suck it, Mitch.

Stepstompstep! Stepstompstep! At last, we land in formation (STOMP!), and I raise my hands over my head in exultation. 'Cause I know we did pretty awesome. Way more awesome than the BarneyClones.

"WELL!" Mr. Tux strides back onstage, looking very pleased with himself even though he hasn't actually done anything particularly spectacular tonight. "Looks like we have a WINNER! The first annual GinormoCon *Guitar Hero Dance Dance Champion* is...JACK CAMDEN! AND PARTNER!!!"

The crowd roars with approval. And I finally allow myself to look at Jack. His cheeks are flushed, his eyes wild. His glasses are propped onto his face at a crazy angle, having been jostled all over the damn place during our routine. And he's looking at me like I have just given birth to a Cylon hybrid baby right there onstage.

"What..." he sputters. "How..."

I shrug, reaching up and adjusting his glasses back into place. "Now you know my mutant power."

He smiles then, a full-on beaming grin that makes his eyes crinkle up at the corners. It's not the cheesezoid "I'm a TV star" grin or the teasing "let me show you my mad vid skills" grin or the pained "Claire Yardley sucks" grin. It softens the sharp planes of his face, rendering them less sculpted, less refined. I realize then that I'm standing very close to him, closer than I have since...well. You know. He smells like sweat and soap and I'm all hot-cold again and I can't seem to look away from that smile. And as my eyes wander over his face, they are drawn to a faint, milky-pale crescent near the left corner of his mouth. A scar. A non-perfect, non-geometric element. Weird. They must cover it up with makeup for the sho—oh. *Oh.*

Suddenly, I remember. My brain rewinds, sorting through the bleary bits and arranging them into one clear image. We're sitting on the couch of my hotel room. I'm sinking into its depths, alcohol percolating in my brain, wondering if the cushions are going to swallow me whole. I feel like I'm made of liquid, my head flopping to one side as I try to focus on this strange person next to me. His body is angled toward mine, his arm hanging lazily over the armrest. He's telling me about how it's so easy to feel lost sometimes. And alone and weak and *stupid*. That's what he was trying to tell me earlier…you know, about that *Periodic Seven* storyline with Glory Gilmore? Issues 10 through 14? It just came out wrong. It always does. His features are so defined, so larger-than-life, as he speaks. I try to concentrate on one at a time. Eyes…blue, blue, blue. "Blue" is kind of a funny word. Mouth, stretching across his face, his amazingly symmetrical…wait. There's a ghostly, crooked half-moon tracing a tiny path right next to his mouth. He notices me squinting at it.

Big Wheel accident, he explains. When I was six.

Something about that stabs straight to my heart.

I lean into him, placing my hands on his chest. My lips brush his earlobe as I tell him about Glory Gilmore. About always losing her. About how Curtis stealing The Last Glory seems like such a small thing, such a small, stupid thing. But it *wasn't*. It just wasn't, you know? It was fucking *important*. Issues 10 through 14 were my favorites, too. I've never met anyone else who loves those issues…who even likes them.

That's how I feel, I say. That's how I always feel. Issues 10 through 14.

And then I dig my fingernails into the back of his neck and pull him close, crushing his mouth with mine.

I am yanked back into the present by another deafening cheer. Mr. Tux has just gifted us with our amazing prize… "—a free CASE OF RED BULLLLL!"

"Go ahead and donate that to our fellow partygoers," Jack tells him. He gives a final wave to the crowd, grabs my hand and leads me offstage. I follow him in a daze.

When we hit the party floor, he starts running, pulling me along like a lead-filled caboose. We run through the hall and out the door, escaping into night. I lean against a handy convention-center pillar, winded. He starts jumping around like a maniac.

"That was AWE! SOME!!" he cries, pumping a fist in the air. "So fucking cool. I wonder if we can come back next year and defend our title? Maybe if we—"

"Jack," I finally croak.

He snaps to attention. "What?" he says, going all serious. "Are you okay?" He crosses over to me, his eyes searching mine. One of his hands—those nice hands—cups my face, his thumb tracing a gentle path down my cheek.

My back is still glued to the pillar. It props me up, allows me to meet his gaze.

"I remember."

This time, he kisses me first.

Once again, I am awakened extremely rudely. My cell phone buzzes for attention, skittering across the nightstand like a hyperactive insect.

"Mrph. Don't get that," Jack murmurs into my neck. I am, however, fairly sure he's technically still asleep, so I carefully remove the arm that's draped over my hip and ease myself into a seated position, flipping open the bug-phone.

"Hello?"

"Julie?"

"Mitch! What's with the wake-up ca—"

"It's Braidbeard," he interrupts, his voice tense. "He's in big trouble. You have to...you have to help him. You're his only hope."

– PART III –
JUST A GIRL

CHRIS ROCK

IN

I THINK
I LOVE
MY WIFE

ONLY IN THEATRES
MARCH 2007

Schmthulu

June 10, 2009

No one remembers how *The Periodic Seven* ended.

And by "no one," I mean "the five people who clung stubbornly to the book as it thrashed its final death throes and faded into dusty quarter-bin obscurity."

Yes, I was one of those people. Shut up.

In the climactic story arc, the team faces off against Monstrovore, a gigantic, tentacled beast genetically engineered by Doctor Halogen. Said creature paralyzes its foes by invoking an amorphous sort of dread—a nameless, faceless horror—in their very souls. For three wretched issues, it tortures the Seven, forcing them to confront their worst fears, face their angst-laden demons, blah blah, a shitload of flashbacks and dream sequences, blah blah.

So how do they defeat this monster, this looming threat to their sanity and their lives and civilization as we fucking know it?

They don't.

Instead, Monstrovore picks them off one by one, and we watch our heroes die a series of increasingly gratuitous deaths, ultimately disappearing into the filthy basement of forgotten comic book history.

I know. I *know*. It's a completely batshit-insane detour into Shark-Jumping Crazyland, only it's more like this particular storyline clears the shark and keeps running and then trips over a few random potholes before blazing off into the distance, cackling maniacally and flipping everyone—fans! Marvel!—the bird.

At the time, I had no Lovecraftian frame of reference, so I didn't realize that good ol' Monstro was basically a bargain-basement take on a Cthulhuesque creation—a Schmthulu, of sorts. But you know what? Schmthulu fucking *terrified me*. I was nine. I didn't know about comic book sales figures and cancellations and vindictive writers who decide to send their doomed titles off in a blaze of something resembling dubious glory. All I knew was that this was the one thing Glory Gilmore couldn't defeat, the one evil she couldn't conquer.

In my adult years, all of my irrational fears have taken on a Schmthulu sort of mantle. Whenever I feel a stab of out-of-nowhere terror—like, for example, the night after I saw *The Grudge* and was afraid to cross my apartment building's courtyard because I suddenly thought the big-mouthed cat boy was going to jump out from behind the stairwell and *kill me* and yes, this was the American version, I can't even bring myself to watch the "real" one, fuck you —I imagine Schmthulu rising up inside of me, threatening to swallow me whole. And that's when I've gotta step up and do a little Buffy-esque posturing and kick his/her/its ass, for the sake of maintaining my own carefully calibrated equilibrium.

And for Glory Gilmore, who couldn't fight back in the end.

—Posted on GloryGilmoreLives.com

July 19, 2009
9:48 a.m. Or "when hell froze over."

"You're his only hope."

I sound these words out, trying to rearrange them into a formation that actually makes sense.

"Are you still there?!" Mitch's voice blares through the phone, high-pitched and strained and very un-Mitch-like. He sounds like a Pokemon trainer, or maybe Linn Minmei in pre-concert stress mode.

"I...hold on." I plant my feet on the floor and push off from the bed, woozily trying to figure out my next step. Clothes. I need clothes. I blearily survey the dirt-colored carpet. There do seem to be a lot of clothes here, but I'm not entirely sure which ones are mi—

"JULIEEEEEEE!"

Even though the hand holding the phone has dropped to my side, well away from ear-range, I can still hear Mitch's insistent squawk. I cover the mouthpiece.

After a few seconds of dazedly scanning the room, I snag the piece of apparel that seems closest to me—Jack's semi-infamous Doctor Strange shirt—and slide it over my head. Phone clutched purposefully in my right hand, I slip into the bland, Holiday Inn-ified bathroom, shut the door, and perch myself on the edge of the tub.

"Okay...what?" I hiss, bringing the phone back to my ear. "And also... what?!?"

"Braidbeard's in trouble..."

"You said that part. I want to know about the *other* part."

Mitch lets out a gusty sigh. "Okay. Let me back up. Remember his interview with Graham Barrett?"

"You mean the one he lorded over me while I was wallowing in my hangover?"

Another sigh. "Yeah. So...it didn't go so well. Graham's personal publicist gave B a list of taboo topics—stuff he was specifically not supposed to ask about, like personal life shit and spoiler shit."

"Wait." I groan. "I can see where this is going."

"Yeah. So, as you've probably gathered, one of those taboo topics was the movie version of *Solar Knights*. Which, if you'll remember, Graham denounced from the beginning and has refused to speak of ever since."

"Can't blame him," I mutter. "It was so fucking bad—Uwe Boll bad. And let me guess: Braidbeard just couldn't contain himself."

"That's about right," Mitch says ruefully. "He asked the question. And Mr. Barrett, having a reputation of glorious bastardism to maintain, went apeshit, which set off a chain reaction. His publicist freaked on Kirstie and Kirstie freaked on B."

"Okay, I'm still not seeing where the crisis is," I say, trying to tug the insufficient t-shirt over my backside. "It's Sunday. We have precious few con hours left. Won't everyone have forgotten about this by the time the next one rolls around?"

"Well...that's the problem." Mitch hesitates. "She put him on The List."

"Mitch..." I shake my head. "Come on. There's no such thing."

The List is an urban con legend of epic proportions. It is said to contain the names of journalists who have, for various reasons, been banned for life from the convention circuit. Not just one convention in particular, mind you: it is supposedly circulated amongst the flacks for cons worldwide. If you're on The List, your days of marinating in rehashed genre celebrity witticisms and junket-provided Coca-Cola products are over. To me, this has always had the whiff of a wild-eyed, all-caps "J.J. ABRAMS DIRECTS TEH STAR TREKS!!!"-type message board rumor. But then, look how that turned out.

"He's on it," Mitch says firmly. "They took away his credentials, his badge—everything. And Kirstie warned him about showing up at DragonCon."

"Okay," I say. I pluck a wax-paper-wrapped soap bar from the corner of the tub and turn it over in my hand, scrutinizing the perfectly folded corners. "So he fucked up. I still don't see how I can help, here."

"Julie." Mitch has his ultra-serious voice on. "Kirstie…likes you. She thinks you guys have, like, a bond. I bet if you talked to her, it would really smooth things over."

"What?!" I toss the soap aside, letting it clatter into the bathtub. "You want me to grovel to someone I can't stand, all in the name of helping someone I can't stand *even more*?"

"Well—"

"No. He dug his own fucking grave. It was inevitable that he would, someday. I'm not going out on a limb for someone who repeatedly acts like an ass and thinks there won't be any consequences."

Mitch goes silent for a moment. "You know," he finally says, drawing out each word carefully, "much as you might hate to admit it, the two of you are pretty goddamn similar in a lot of ways."

"Not funny," I snap.

"You're right," he says. "It's not fucking funny. Because there's at least one key difference. He would do this for *you*."

With a staticky "thunk," the line goes dead.

"Well, fuck you, too," I mutter.

I snap the phone closed in one decisive motion. In fact, it is so decisive a motion that I nearly lose my balance and fall ass-backwards into the tub. I stand up shakily, and pull at the t-shirt, trying to give myself just another inch of hemline. Next time I decide to have a contentious, meandering bathroom conversation, I'm gonna put on some pants.

I emerge from my secret telephone lair to find Jack sitting up in bed, awake but not quite alert. He leans back against the headboard, rubbing sleep from his half-lidded eyes.

"Hi," he says, squinting in my general direction. "You're blurry. But I think I love your outfit."

I feel my face flush and bite my lip to keep from smiling. I cross the room, toss my phone on the nightstand, and slide in next to him, t-shirt and all. He puts an arm around me in a way that seems weirdly courtly, like we're at the drive-in movie or the sock hop or something.

"So," he says. "What do you think, Girl Detective? Is this—and by 'this,' I mean completely embarrassing yourself in a *Dance Dance Revolution* tournament—the best con experience ever?"

I angle my body toward his, tentatively resting my head on his shoulder. I suddenly feel as if I'm enveloped in a protective bubble—a chintzy *Get Smart*-ian gadget, plastic and fantastic, holding me slightly apart from him, everything still and perfect and close to the bone. My own Cone of Shyness.

Which is, you know, kind of weird, considering how Not!Shy we both were just a few hours ago.

His fingertips wander away from my shoulder, grazing the back of my neck. An army of rebellious goosebumps marches its merry way through the general area. I don't even know. Obviously, the Cone of Shyness is fucking defective.

"Embarrassing?" I finally say, attempting to feign outrage. "I *shredded*. I probably could have won that shit all by my lonesome."

"Probably," he says. "But remember: my virtuosic *Guitar Hero* star powering got you there in the first place. Never forget the little people in your quest for complete and total arcade dominance."

He grins at me, his eyes teasing, yet still a little lazy and clouded with sleep. My gut flutters, a bizarre brew of exhilaration and total fucking nausea. For one manic moment, I imagine myself bolting through the hotel halls, jumping up and down exuberantly, then collapsing to the ground and puking all over myself.

Maybe this is another symptom of that weird-ass flu.

"By the way," he continues, "I wanted to pick up on something extremely important we were discussing before Claire...you know, interrupted."

"What's that?" I tilt my head, smiling at him gamely.

"The Many Assembled Theories of Julie," he intones, infusing each word with faux-dramatic flair. "Do you, in fact, have one for every major issue to ever plague geekdom, and if so, can I please hear some more?"

"Okay," I say, arranging my face into a mock-serious expression. "Topic?"

"Organic webshooters."

"A reasonable reinvention of a classic device, and certainly not worth the shitload of fanboy tantrum-throwing that ensued."

"*Deep Space Nine.*"

"The superior *Trek* in every way. And anyone who prefers *Babylon* fucking *5* isn't worth talking to."

"Buffy Summers' ultimate soulmate."

"Angel."

"What?!" he looks genuinely surprised. "*You* would pick Angel?"

"I'm cookie dough." I grin at him, deciding to leave it at that.

"Huh." He shakes his head bemusedly. "So your romantic nature extends beyond Cyclops/Phoenix 'shipping. I like that."

"Shut up." I nudge him the ribs.

"Okay, okay," he says. "Is there anything you want to quiz me on in return? I don't have as extensive a library of well-considered nerd talking points as you do, but it's only fair."

"Hmm," I say. "Well, given the wide range of geek events you probably go to and the mass amounts of alcohol at said events...I still don't quite buy that this is your first con-quest." I raise an eyebrow. "Surely there have been others?"

I expect him to get a chuckle out of my oh-so-clever terminology, but instead, he tilts his head to the side and looks at me intently. I notice that his hair is sticking out comically in the back, pillow-mussed into a vaguely pyramid-like formation. "No," he says softly.

I tear my gaze from his, twisting the end of the bed sheet around my finger. That exuberant/pukey feeling is just *raging*.

"Oh, hey," he says, perhaps sensing my recurrent urge to vomit and affecting a more casual cadence, "why are you getting urgent phone calls so early in the morning? Hot scoop?"

"Hardly," I say. I briefly recount the tale of Braidbeard and the Pissed-Off Brit.

"It's just...dumb," I conclude lamely. "Mitch and I don't really fight. I dunno." The final moments of our phone call flicker through my brain and I flinch a little.

Jack nods thoughtfully, giving my shoulder a reassuring squeeze. "You know..." he says. "In our limited time together last night, I did kind of get the impression that you and Braidbeard were...um, friends."

"Well, we're not," I say. "We're more like...arch-enemies who occasionally come together for a mutually beneficial goal. Like Professor X and Magneto."

"Wouldn't helping him out this time sort of be...that?" he asks, brow furrowing. "Like you'd be maintaining the balance on the con circuit and preserving the sanctity of your mighty—if slightly dysfunctional—trio?"

"Why are you so bent on taking Mitch's side?" My shoulders tense and I suddenly feel as if I'm positioned in the most uncomfortable way possible. Like a puppet whose strings are being yanked, I lift my head from Jack's shoulder and sit up straight. "I mean, he basically implied that I'm... I'm...some sort of unfeeling, bitch-faced automaton." I train my eyes on my lap. "Do you think that, too?"

"No, of course not. But..." He hesitates, then speaks carefully. "You have this thing where...you kind of *want* people to think that."

The words hang in the air. Something about them is so precise, so weighted and specific, they echo through my head and lodge themselves in my brain, repeating and repeating and repeating.

My chest tightens. I swallow hard, trying to clamp down on the wild thread of desperation worming its way through my gut. "Since when do you know me well enough to comment on...my *things*?" I say. It comes out sharp and spiteful, a harsh exclamation point of a statement.

Surprise registers in his eyes, then confusion. "Hey," he says gently. He reaches over and brushes an unruly clump of hair out of my eyes. "I didn't mean..."

"Oh, I think you did," I say, my voice colder than I intend it to be. "Just say what you want to say, Jack."

He leans back against the headboard and lets out an exasperated sigh, his face slowly clouding over.

"Fine," he says after a tense moment, his tone low and firm. "You want me to be honest? Your whole deal has been pretty obvious to me since the moment we met."

"What is that supposed to mean?"

He gives me a look that's unnerving in its directness. "It means you're really fucking scared."

A wave of blinding frustration engulfs me, robbing me of my ability to form a single coherent thought. Not even LiveJulie is coming to my rescue. "*I'm* scared?" I say, my voice shaking dangerously. "You're the one who… who hides."

"How's that?" His voice is like ice.

"Your whole…" I gesture limply. "Persona. Nod, smile. Sound bites and schmooze. Be what they want you to be. But don't even *think* about showing anyone who you really are."

He frowns, a dull flash of sadness drifting over his face. "I showed *you*," he says quietly.

I crumple the edge of the sheet in my fist and shake my head vehemently, as if such forceful acts will give me some modicum of control over the situation. "This…this is why I don't do…stuff like this."

"Right," he snaps. He pushes himself out of bed, pacing the room feverishly. He's clad only in out-of-season, holiday-themed boxers with reindeer and snowmen all over them. The sheer ridiculousness of this juxtaposition magnifies his anger in a weird way, makes it more pointed. He finally comes to an abrupt halt, crossing his arms over his chest and frowning at me.

"I *like* you," he says. It almost sounds like an accusation.

"Well, I really don't know *why*," I growl. "Considering what a scared, heartless bitch I am."

He exhales sharply, raking a hand through his hair. The rickety hair-pyramid shifts to one side, but remains standing. "Because…" he says. "Because when you're not obsessing over maintaining your carefully crafted 'I'm above this shit' persona, when you're not walling yourself up in the Fortress of Emotional Solitude, when you're just being *you*...you're pretty fucking cool."

He tilts his head, his gaze boring into me. "But apparently, all of that is impossible for you to deal with. Accepting actual, non-automaton feelings means giving up a teeny, tiny bit of control, and you can't do that...can you?"

Those last two words come out plaintive, an almost hopeful question that evaporates into the air between us.

I stare at him for a moment. The tension has fled my body and I feel like I'm wilting into the soft, creaky mattress. His eyes hold mine. They really are ridiculously blue.

Suddenly, I want so badly to say something, to say anything, to somehow take us back to where we were five minutes ago. But the words won't come. Because I know he's right. Because I *can't*.

I hug my arms to my chest and turn away. Out of the corner of my eye, I see him look down at the floor, as if trying to memorize every tiny flaw of the hideous carpet, every cigarette burn and loose fiber.

Finally he says, "I need to go."

I don't say anything. I don't try to stop him as he slowly pulls on his clothes, claps his hand over his back jeans pocket to make sure his wallet's there, and heads for the door. I sit mutely in bed, twisting the sheet into different formations, examining my nails, occasionally staring out the window. I keep expecting him to turn back and look at me as he's leaving, but he doesn't.

An hour later, I'm finally trudging through the con center. My messenger bag thumps rhythmically against my hip, dragging my overloaded shoulder down with every footfall.

I stop in a quiet expanse of hall near one of the stairways, a section with floor-to-ceiling windows that look out onto the city. This, truthfully, is one of my favorite parts of the convention center: not the jam-packed dealers' area, not the sweaty panel room where everyone piles in eagerly, awaiting two hours of impressive, expletive-laden Kevin Smith monologuing. Here, you can sit on the floor-level window ledge and eat your shitty hot dog and read your battered back issues and feel like the stomach-churning energy of GinormoCon isn't going to knock you flat on your ass.

I stare out the window for a moment, calculating how many hours I have to endure before I can leave for the airport. As I turn away, preparing to enter the fray, a figure sitting on the ledge several windows to the left catches my eye. He's hunched over, eyes downcast and just slightly catatonic-looking. And his scraggly braids are even scragglier than usual.

I sigh. Figures.

I trudge over and plop myself down next to him. We share a moment of heavy silence.

Finally, I say it.

"Braidbeard. What the fuck were you thinking?"

He looks up, blinking slowly, as if coming out of a trance. "I...I just wanted to know." His nasal tones are muted, almost thoughtful. "And it would have been such an awesome scoop. I would've gotten linked everywhere...I'd be the one who got him to talk about it."

"It's just...it seems like such a risk," I say. "Graham Barrett doesn't exactly have the most cuddly reputation."

"I know, I guess I didn't...think about that. I just thought, if I can get in there, if I can get the interview and ask the question..." he trails off.

I nod. I suppose thinking critically—thinking beyond whether something "suxxors" or "pwns"—is probably not Braidbeard's most developed skill. Then again, it would seem that it's not really mine, either.

"I talked to Reg," he says abruptly. Reg is CinePlanet's scowly editor-in-chief. "He said...he said it's cool. He said maybe it's time for me to tackle another beat. Like music or something." His words are matter-of-fact, but his voice quavers.

I picture Braidbeard amongst the heaving throngs at the Warfield, mixed in with vintage-swathed hipsters, aging punks, and legions of bored girls wearing non-prescription cat-eye specs. I see him, notepad in hand, too-big Wolverine t-shirt hanging off his spindly frame, attempting to look unimpressed. I visualize him being jostled from side-to-side by a gaggle of uncaring Ethan Hawke look-alikes in moth-eaten bowling shirts, all trying to get into the groove of a band they claim is "overrated."

I suddenly want to punch them all in the face.

"Wait here for a second," I say.

If it's at all possible, the Media Holding Area looks even more depressing than usual in the waning hours of the con. A few disheveled journalists are draped over folding chairs, comparing back issue finds and "I was so drunk..." stories. A general air of desperation and finality hangs in the stagnant air. This is it. Until next time.

I spot Kirstie flitting about, clipboard in hand. I march over and tap her on the shoulder. She whirls around, beaming. "Jules! You're still here!" Inexplicably, Kirstie seems to have just as much energy now as she did at the beginning of this thing. Her hair tower is as flawless as usual, and her mask of makeup doesn't appear to have budged since I last saw her. Maybe this is *her* mutant power. Or maybe she just overdoses on NoDoz.

"Yeah, you know me—in it 'til the end. Listen, Kirstie. I heard that something happened with my...er, pal, Braidbeard?"

Her face goes a little Dark Phoenix-y and she frowns. I almost expect her eyes to blacken, obliterating the pupils. "What a mess," she says. "I know *you* would never do anything like that, Jules. It's a serious infraction."

"Of course," I say, in what I hope is a soothing voice. "But...I really don't think he meant any harm. He's just really passionate, you know? He's a huge fan of Graham's work, and well...he probably just got a little over-enthusiastic."

She shakes her head, still frowning. "I just can't have the talent upset," she says. "It's important for them to feel like GinormoCon is a super-fun experience."

"Right," I say. "But I know Braidbeard really well and I'm sure this is a one-time thing. He's learned his lesson. It's just...he really loves this stuff. He fits in here in a way that he doesn't fit in anywhere else."

Kirstie cocks her head and looks at me quizzically. I realize that dragging out the violins probably isn't the way to go with her.

"Look," I say, "if you could maybe just reinstate his credentials and take him off The List—with the understanding that he'll never interview Graham Barrett again—you would be doing *me* a huge favor. Whaddya say...er, girlfriend?"

The shift is immediate. The Dark Phoenix visage vanishes into the ether, and suddenly, Kirstie is grinning at me like I've just suggested we go chug cosmos and pick up inappropriate men together. "Well..." she says. "I guess it'll probably blow over by the next con, anyway. What the heck! Oh, but Jules—there's no 'List,' okay?" She winks at me broadly.

"Right," I say, trying to approximate a stagey wink of my own. "Of course."

We stand there for a moment, frozen in a state of smiley awkwardness. "Um...Kirstie," I finally say, "maybe at the next con, we could...have lunch. Or get a drink or something."

Her grin gets wider, straining the corners of her cheeks. The effect is Jokerishly unsettling, yet I feel a tiny surge of affection. "That would be fabulous," she says. "Two crazy gals on the con circuit—you and me!"

"You and me," I agree.

For once, Braidbeard has actually listened to me and is still perched on the exact same window ledge, affecting the exact same hunched-over slouch. Either that, or he's just too beaten down to move. Mitch has joined him and appears to be attempting the pep talk thing.

"…the music scene in the Bay is awesome, B," I hear him say as I stride into earshot. "I can go with you to the shows—it'll be cool."

"Fuck that," I say. "You don't want to hang out with those posers." I toss Braidbeard's laminated press badge into his lap and sit down next to Mitch.

Their heads swivel in my direction so fast, I swear I hear a little "whoosh" sound effect. Braidbeard gawps at me, then looks down at his badge. He holds it up to the light, as if unconvinced it's the real thing.

"How…" he says reverently.

I shrug. "I talked to Kirstie. You're off the hook, but don't be trying to interview His Excellency—aka Lord Barrett—anytime soon. Also, you fucking owe me."

Mitch presses his lips together tightly and stares at his sneakers. I can tell he's trying not to laugh.

Braidbeard stops stroking his badge for a moment and fixes me with an uber-serious gaze. "Anything," he says solemnly. "It's a debt I intend to repay."

"Okay, okay, no need to make things…weird," I say. "Why don't you take that and go cover something."

He nods vigorously and hops up, braids swinging to and fro. "I need to catch the *Stargate* panel—I want to ask Ben Browder if there's any truth to the rumors about a *Farscape* movie. Personally, I think they sound *completely farfetched*, but my readers will just *die* if I don't at least ask the question. But I guess I'll see you guys at the *Periodic Seven* panel later?"

"Maybe," I say neutrally. "I'm thinking of cutting out early."

"Whatevs," he snorts, finally regaining a little of his usual bravado. "I know you've got more stamina than *that*."

And then he's off, racing down the hall, disappearing into the crowd of similarly bespectacled fanfolk.

Mitch watches him go, then turns back to me, raising a quizzical eyebrow. "That was nice of you," he says.

I lean my head against the window, watching the mass of people stream in and out of the con center, identical plastic swag bags clutched in hand. "Is that so weird?" I say. "For me to do something nice?"

He studies me for a moment, then turns to look out the window, taking in the parade of plastic-bag lemmings. "Why aren't you going to the *Periodic Seven* panel?" he asks.

"I'm tired," I say. Truth. "I want to go home."

He nods slowly. We watch as, down on the street, a civvies-clad congoer gets her picture snapped with a pair of Jack Sparrows. One is more convincing than the other, who hasn't even bothered with the eyeliner.

"Where's Jack? Camden, that is," he says, tilting his head toward the twin Sparrow tableau.

I shrug. "I don't think that's gonna work out."

"And why is that?"

I try to brush him off with another shrug. He lets that hang for a moment, then reaches over and lightly places a hand on my arm. "Julie."

I abruptly turn from the window, shaking him off in the process, and lean forward, resting my elbows on my knees. I fix my gaze on the carpet, like it's the one I'm talking to. "It was never going to work out," I say, motoring through the words, trying to get them out as fast as humanly possible. "It was a supremely stupid idea—not even an idea, really. More like an...*impulse*. It's better that it didn't go any farther than it did."

"Okay," he says. "I'm not even sure what 'it' is in this scenario, but okay. Great, fantastic. I'm glad you're so satisfied." He lets out an exasperated sigh. Out of the corner of my eye, I see him run a hand over his forehead, as if trying to stave off a particularly inevitable migraine. "What the fuck is wrong with you?"

My head snaps up. "What?"

"You heard me."

"I...nothing. I mean, I just like to keep things simple."

"Right. Let me translate the technobabble and put this in layman's terms for you. I'm Geordi and you're Counselor Troi."

I open my mouth to object, but he holds up a warning hand. "Shields," he says. "With you, it's always shields. Human interaction that's more complex than banter? Fucking shields *up*, Captain!"

"So it's either shields or a Fortress of Solitude," I mutter. "Awesome."

Mitch ignores me, bent on his rant. "And at the end of the day, those shields really work for ya. Because here you are, arguing with me via rapidly disintegrating *Star Trek* metaphors when you could be spending time with a guy who entered a fucking *Guitar Hero* contest just to impress you."

"It's not...it's not like that," I sputter. To my horror, my voice cracks. I swallow hard as rogue tears prick my eyeballs.

He softens a little. "Then what's it like?"

I take a deep breath, trying to think of the right words. "I like what I like," I say slowly. "I like sticking with Marvel titles even after they've crossed into the realm of undeniable Liefeldian badness. I like arguing with you about why Donna Noble trumps both Martha and Rose as The Doctor's companion..."

He looks like he wants to protest, but I forge on, motormouthed and unstoppable. "I like going home and knowing exactly which TV shows I'm going to watch and in what order. And while I'm watching TV, I like looking at spoiler shit on the 'net, because I like knowing what's going to happen next. And this whole weekend—not just Jack, but all of it, the drinking and the Dance Dancing and the, I don't know, *bonding* with Braidbeard...I feel like it doesn't go with what I like. It doesn't go with *me*." I prop my chin on my fist, staring contemplatively into space.

Mitch nods thoughtfully, taking in my verbal spew. We sit for a moment in weighted silence.

"Um, so Layla and I are dating."

I whip around to look at him. "What? You mean you finally asked her out?"

"No." His eyes shift back and forth. "We've been, um, seeing each other for a few months."

My jaw drops and all I can do is gape, my own problems momentarily forgotten. "You...why didn't you tell me?" I finally squawk.

"Because we've been trying to keep it quiet, see where it goes." He rakes a hand through his hair. "And because, Julie...you make everything so damn *difficult*."

"But...I've been, you know, encouraging you. To date her."

"I know. But I didn't know how you would feel if I...*actually* dated her. You...it's like you said. You like when things stay the same. When they're exactly what you expect. And if I suddenly can't make *Spaced* marathon night because I have a date with my girlfriend...well, that's probably *not* what you're expecting."

I frown, open my mouth and close it. I can't think of what to say to that. I turn back to the floor.

"You're my best friend," I finally murmur. "You're, like...my only friend."

"And you're mine," he says. "But you're also the world's biggest pain in the ass."

I bite my lip, staring at the carpet. Suddenly, I'm thinking about cutting a few of those Marvel titles from my pull list.

He lets out an exasperated sigh, reaches over, and clamps his hands on my shoulders, turning me so I'm facing him.

"Julie," he says, stretching the second syllable out a bit. "If the way you're doing things now is all perfect, why are you so upset? You get to go back to living exactly the way you want to in just a few short hours."

I look at him blankly.

"What do you want?" he asks gently. "Don't overthink it, just say the first thing that pops into your head. Right now, this moment: what do you want?"

As my brain slowly absorbs the question, I'm overloaded with images. Blue eyes, divulging the mysteries of issues 10 through 14. Sickly-looking sandwiches, lit up in all their vending machine glory. Hair pyramids.

I get a flash of that exhilarated-yet-wanna-vomit sensation and I suddenly realize that it's both the best and the worst feeling I've ever had, that I want to experience it again and again and again, that I can't quite explain its appeal...but it's there. It's a kind of being scared. Not Schmthulu. Something much better.

And I've been avoiding it forever. Because I can't stop attaching stupid amounts of meaning to an act of petty thievery committed by some idiot I never even liked very much in the first place. Because I can't shed all the put-ons and personas I wear every day. Because I can't just *let fucking go*.

And suddenly, I know. I want to stop being afraid in one way so I can be totally fucking freaked out in another. I want...

"...Jack," I say out loud. "I want Jack."

Mitch nods, a slow grin overtaking his face. His eyes are full of pride, like I've finally conceded on the whole Donna-Martha-Rose debate (I never will!).

"Okay," he says, nodding. "Okay. So how can we make that happen?"

"I don't know. I...don't think he wants to talk to me."

Mitch cocks his head to the side, his eyes taking on the undeniable light of a born schemer. He appears lost in thought for a moment. Then: "Give me your bag."

"Uh..."

"Give it to me." I pass him my crammed-to-the-gills messenger tote.

He rummages around, pushing aside leaky pens and battered press kits. Finally, he finds what he's looking for.

"Yes." He grins, brandishing the no longer mint-on-card Glory Gilmore. I forgot she was still hiding out in there.

He rotates her arms above her head, so it looks like she's doing an awkward, stiff-limbed victory dance. "Her powers still blow," he says, eyes twinkling roguishly. "But she came to you for a reason. And I think I know what it is."

I study him, wondering what nefarious plot he's cooking up. "You know, Mitch," I say, "I really like Layla."

"This is so not going to work." I cradle Glory in my sweaty palm. I visualize myself magically transferring my nerves—the inner Schmthulu, currently rearing its ugly, ugly head—into her smooth, plastic form.

"Shhhh." Mitch nudges me. "Don't be a pussy."

"You know, that's really sexist and offensive," I hiss. "And I hate that word."

"Okay," he whispers back. "Don't be a vag—"

"Shut up!" I growl, loudly enough to attract death glares and shushes from the Sailor Moon cosplayers seated directly in front of us.

"Sorry," I murmur.

We're wedged into our chairs in the con center's biggest ballroom. Up front, larger-than-life versions of Jack and Claire Yardley emote their way across a giant screen, enacting a particularly poignant *Periodic Seven* moment. Something about lives lost and trust regained? Oh, fuck, I don't know. I'm too busy freaking out.

I force myself to concentrate on the screen, as if it will lull me into a sense of calm. I study Jack's magnified features. Those eyes that look right through you. That little crinkle he gets in the middle of his forehead when he's concentrating on something. I don't know how I ever thought of him as soulless. Clearly, I wasn't watching this shit closely enough.

The clip ends. As the crowd claps enthusiastically, the panel's moderator strides onstage and oh my fucking God, it's Mr. Tux. Only not wearing a tux. Are those khakis? My mind is seriously blown. "Wasn't that FAN-TASTIC?" He grins toothily. "Let's welcome our panelists!"

They file out to another round of cheers and seat themselves behind the long, microphone-and-water-bottle-cluttered table. Claire is there, as is Rudy James, who plays Doctor Halogen. The show's fortysomething creator, Josh Daniels, plops down between them, his Cubs baseball cap and air of studied slovenliness giving him away as a non-actor. Jack sits on the end, propped up in his chair, head lolling to the side like a deactivated robot's.

Mr. Tux cycles through the standard array of "gosh, this show is neat and maybe tell us what happens next, even though I know you really can't, spoilerzzz!" questions. Josh does most of the talking, lacing his sentences with eminently quotable witticisms. Claire interjects with a flirtatious quip or two, an indulgent smile plastered on her face. Rudy gives rambling answers that somehow encompass evolution, genocide, and the current state of slam poetry as an art form, prompting Josh to interrupt when he can with a smooth, "What I think Rudy's trying to say is..." Jack mostly just nods along.

I squirm the whole time, unable to come to a remotely comfortable seated position. Mitch elbows me. "Relax," he mutters.

Finally, Mr. Tux opens the floor to audience questions, inviting crowd members to form a line at the microphone up front.

"Go," Mitch whispers. He reaches over and gives my free hand—the one not clutching Glory as if she is my only tether to this world—a squeeze. "It'll be okay."

I launch myself out of my seat and bolt up front, managing to secure the third place in line. Josh, Claire, and Rudy gaze at the fans piling in front of the microphone, feigning interest in the imminent barrage of questions. Jack isn't even trying—his eyes are downcast, and he's staring intently at his water bottle, as if it's going to offer him some Guardian of Forever-esque platitudes. He doesn't see me.

Fan #1 has a long, complicated question that seems to involve the show's continuity as it relates to actual physics. Josh does his best to answer, then jokingly asks if she'd like a job as technical adviser. She has the good grace to laugh it off. Fan #2 wants to sing a song he composed especially for Claire. "Isn't that sweeeeet," she coos when it's over, bringing her palms together in a delicate golf clap.

And then, the microphone is staring me right in the face. I feel my heart slamming into my breastbone, and I picture it popping out of my chest, going all 3-D and cartoony, like I'm Pepe Le Pew and I've just spotted that stupid cat who can't seem to avoid errant cans of white paint. I tighten my grip on Glory and try to let Mitch's words echo through my head, Yoda-like and zen-ifying: *It'll be okay.*

"Um," I clear my throat. My voice sounds so loud, reverberating through the mic. "I have a question for Jack."

His head snaps up and he spots me, his eyes going all big.

"Well...go ahead, then, young lady!" Mr. Tux says jovially. I can't believe he doesn't recognize me from my stunning victory the night before. Whatever, Mr. Tux.

"Well, actually...it's more like a, um, gift," I say.

"Okaaaaaaaaay." Mr. Tux raises a suspicious eyebrow, undoubtedly anticipating that I am about to proffer a lock of my hair, a portable Travis

Trent shrine, or worst of all, a script. "Well, I'm afraid we don't usually allow—"

"It's okay," Jack interjects. His voice is hoarse, but firm. He meets my gaze, his eyes full of questions, and gives me a little nod.

I propel myself forward to the stage. The top of the table is at forehead level, so I raise myself onto my tiptoes and set Glory's plastic form in front of Jack. I keep my eyes trained downward. I can't look at him.

My task completed, I turn on my heel and hurry away, bypassing my seat next to Mitch and opting to stand in the very back.

"Well, uh...thank you," says Mr. Tux. "Why don't we move on to the next question?"

The next fan in line asks about the long-rumored movie adaptation of the show. Josh starts to answer, but I tune him out. I can only focus on the silent figure at the end of the table as he turns Glory over in his hands, his face blank.

God. Why did I let Mitch talk me into this?

Then he sees it. The tiny note, the folded scrap of paper attached to her foot. He looks puzzled for a moment, then tugs it free and starts to unfold it, his brow furrowed. My way-too-loud heartbeat roars in my ears. Oh, *frak*. I can't take it anymore.

I push through the ballroom doors and run.

I don't know where I'm running to. The corridors seem endless, a ridiculous maze of mellow blues and greens and off-whites appropriate for any manner of corporate event. At some point, I hazily realize that I left my bag in the panel room. Oh well. I'm sure they'll let me on the plane with no...ID. I'm sure! I'll just explain the whole story and that'll be that! Who wouldn't let me on the plane after hearing my sordid tale of sex and woe and fandom?!

I finally see stairs. Oh, good. Stairs are good! Stairs lead DOWN. Down and fucking outta here! I clatter down the stairs and keep running. I see the food court bouncing into view, that sickening not-quite-food smell filling my nostrils.

And in that moment, I suddenly become aware of a vaguely thunderous sound behind me, getting louder and louder and louder. I screech to a halt in front of the food court and whip around, breathing hard.

And there's Jack. He's running, just like I was only seconds ago, and he skids to a stumbling stop in front of me, doubling over, trying to catch his breath. I open my mouth, hoping to make words come out, but I'm frozen in shock. And it only gets worse when I look up. Because apparently, that thunderous sound was courtesy of the whole goddamn panel audience sprinting through the con center en masse, hot on Jack's heels, a supremely nerdy tribute to the running of the bulls.

They all stop when he does, practically in unison. The effect would be hilarious if it wasn't so...well, *insane.* I scan the crowd. I see Mitch and Braidbeard and Layla, craning their necks to get a better view. I see Josh and Rudy (no Claire, but then, she probably can't run in her skyscraper heels). I see Mr. Tux, looking none too pleased that his panel has apparently been completely hijacked.

Jack finally straightens up, his breathing evening out. He takes a step toward me. I still can't move.

"What...what are you doing?" I finally manage, my voice twisting up at the end like a deranged chipmunk's.

"I'm chasing you," he says. His face is flushed, but his tone is mild and his eyes are hooded, revealing nothing.

"What are *they* doing?" I gesture to the crowd.

"WE FOLLOWED HIM!" someone yells.

"Mr. Camden decided to leave the panel right after you presented him with your...gift," says Mr. Tux, his voice dripping with disdain. "Even though we technically still have fifteen minutes left."

"HE JUMPED OVER THE TABLE," someone hollers. "I TWITTED IT!"

"THE CORRECT TERM IS TWEETED!" someone else retorts.

I turn back to Jack, feeling like I might keel over at any second. He produces a white scrap of paper from his pocket—my note—and holds it up questioningly.

I am suddenly excruciatingly aware of the hush that's fallen over the crowd assembled around us. I feel twin flames bloom on my cheeks and tug self-consciously at my hair, which is at its most disastrous and antennae-like after my unanticipated bout of physical activity. "Jack," I whisper. "Can we go somewhere more...private?"

He takes another step toward me, closing most of the gap between us so that we're nearly toe to toe. "No," he says. His eyes are still guarded, but one side of his mouth turns up in a lopsided grin.

"Okay," I say crossly. "Fine."

I hesitate, trying to remember everything I wanted to say. Oh, fuck it. This situation isn't really lending itself to impeccable speechifying.

"This weekend has been really...weird for me," I say. "I feel like I've been a complete fucking freak the entire time."

"LOUDER!" someone yells.

"WE CAN'T HEAR YOU!" another heckler chimes in.

"She said she's a FREAK," Jack calls out helpfully.

"And," I continue, trying not to get rattled, "you were right. I am scared of a lot of things. You know...human-feeling-type things."

Over Jack's shoulder, I spot my friends, who have managed to elbow their way to the front of the pack. Mitch and Layla exchange a meaningful lovey-dovey look. Braidbeard gives me a dopey thumbs-up.

I pause. That nameless horror, that senseless dread, thrums through my entire body and I know I must look exactly like Glory Gilmore right before she met her ultimate doom. I scrunch my hands into fists and attempt to summon every ounce of superheroine panache I can muster. I am going to fucking smack you down, Schmthulu. You are nothing but a third-tier, poorly conceived, fucking rip-off piece of shit bad guy and you can go *fuck yourself*. Because I am going to say this next thing. I am. Here we go. I take a deep breath.

"The thought of being with someone absolutely terrifies me. The thought of not seeing you again is...worse."

I scrutinize his face, which has remained fairly expressionless throughout my oration. Complete silence has descended on the crowd, and the con-goers eating in the food court have abandoned their sausage rolls and Starbucks, preferring to gawk at the impromptu Theater of Angst we're putting on.

And then, slowly, that smile—the one I misjudged so much in the beginning, the one that kickstarts that delirious happy-barfy feeling—overtakes his face. There's an added dimension to it this time, an unabashed tenderness that makes those stupid tears well up in my eyes all over again. And before I know what's happening, he's folding me into his arms, pulling me tightly to him, whispering in my ear. And he's saying, "Nice work, Girl Detective."

He pulls back, one arm still encircling my waist, and reaches over with his free hand to smooth my hair-antennae away from my face. Then he tilts down and I tilt up and we meet in the middle, his lips finding mine.

I'm dimly aware that there seems to be some applause going on, maybe an "awww, yeah!" or two. But it fades to a background burble and everything—the grease-drenched food court smells and the stale convention air and just, well, *everything*—falls away and it's just me and him, wrapped in a protective bubble of our own. I guess I don't mind sharing my Cone of Shyness.

We finally break apart, breathless. I smile up at him, and all I can think is that I really want to kiss him again. And maybe do some other things. Did I mention his hands? Because he also has a really nice—

"AHEM."

Dammit, Mr. Tux. You sure do know how to fuck up a nice moment.

"ALRIGHT," bellows Mr. Tux. "Well. What a way to end GINORMOCON! AM I RIGHT?!" The crowd cheers in the affirmative. Mr. Tux looks totally exhausted. "Okay," he mutters. "So let's all move along. Doors close at six."

The crowd starts to dissipate. Food court enthusiasts return to their sausage rolls. Jack and I just stand there for a moment, awkward and shell-shocked. He looks at me thoughtfully.

"What?" I ask, suddenly self-conscious.

A grin pulls at the corners of his mouth. "I *have* to know," he says. "Why Angel?"

I groan, crossing my arms over my chest. "Haven't I made enough substantially embarrassing confessions for one weekend?"

"Please?" he widens his eyes, making them all guileless and Bambiesque. Goddammit.

"Alright," I concede, throwing my hands up in the air. "So you know that crossover episode in season one of *Angel*? 'I Will Remember You'? Angel becomes human and he and Buffy can finally be together and then he realizes that he actually has to go back to being *not* human—you know, for the greater good? So he does, but then Buffy's memory of their one perfect day is wiped out and it's just him all alone with this tragic knowledge and this total fucking sacrifice?"

"I seem to remember such an episode," he says.

"Okay," I say. "That episode always makes me cry."

He cocks his head to the side, eyes dancing with amusement. "That's it?"

"That's it. Angel wins."

He nods, as if this makes more sense than anything else in the world. "Seems reasonable," he says.

He reaches into his back pocket and produces the six inches of plastic that brought us together. Glory Gilmore. He presses her into my hand.

"She's yours," he says. "She always was."

I study her for a moment. Her tiny arms are still raised in victory. "I know," I say. "But I've been thinking. Maybe you could take care of her for me. And then I could come visit...her. In L.A. Sometime."

"Oh, yeah?" He gives me a slow smile and my heart rattles around my chest like a pinball in a machine.

"Yeah," I say. "After all, I would need to make sure you weren't slackin' off. Looking after somebody else's action figures is serious business."

He holds out his hand. I pass her back to him and he tucks her in his pocket, then reaches over and laces his fingers through mine. We stroll toward the big glass doors, away from the last gasps of GinormoCon insanity. "You know," I say hesitantly. "I may be the freak, but you're kind of going without cloaking devices here, too. What with the…table-jumping and the PDA and all. Not very sound bitey."

"I guess you bring it out in me," he says, grinning. He squeezes my hand, then waggles his eyebrows at me in a way that's probably supposed to be borderline lecherous, but is mostly just dorkily endearing. "So. You have an hour or two to spare before you catch your plane?"

I look down at our intertwined fingers, feel the warmth of his palm against mine, and squint into the sun as we pass through the doors and emerge onto the street, surrounded by the endless rush of wiped-out conventioneers. And I say, "I've got time."

EXTRAS

The One Con Glory cast reveals their...

Favorite *Buffy* Episodes

Julie: "Helpless"

Buffy gets all de-powered and shit. The parental stuff with Giles is totally moving, but the most devastating moment is when our girl wonders what she has to offer the world beyond Slayer mojo. "If I'm not the Slayer...why would you like me?" she asks Angel, voice all small and quivery. If that doesn't make you start bawling your head off, I don't want to talk to you. Also, this eppy marks the first appearance of Harris Yulin—so amazing in *Deep Space Nine*'s "Duet"—as a rather persnickety Watcher. He's a fucking genre rock star, you guys.

Jack: "Bewitched, Bothered and Bewildered"

Hmm: pretty, attitude-y girl finally wises up and wears her heart (necklace) on her sleeve? Yeah, I can't imagine why I like this one. No clue.

Mitch: "Family"

I know, I know: you were all expecting "The Zeppo," right? Whatever. I AM NOT A STEREOTYPE. I actually prefer the straight-up heartfelt to the overly meta. Anyway, I really dug the fact that Tara finally got a decent showcase—she may have been the strong, silent type, but she was also the glue holding the Scoobies together. And I think she's mind-blowingly hot. Um, don't tell Layla I said that.

Braidbeard: "Doublemeat Palace"

Why is this much-maligned classic so reviled? Because people are frakking idiots. If you'd all just stop whining for two seconds about how "unrealistic" it is for Buffy to get a job at a fast food joint (like, seriously? And the rest of this show is *totally believable*?), you'd see that "DP" actually offers up an ingenious metaphor pertaining to the state of our increasingly commodified culture. So watch it again, dumbasses.

Layla: "???"

Oooooh! Well...I've only seen, like, two and a half episodes, but the one where everyone sings is so beautiful and amazing and has such pretty clothes and art direction. Bright red lipsticks and corset tops and a lil' ditty about bunnies? I can so get behind that. Oh, and that girl Mitch has a crush on is a fantastic singer!

Author Q&A

Recently, high-profile geek journalist Braidbeard sat down for a chat with *One Con Glory* author Sarah Kuhn. Here's what transpired.

Braidbeard: So how did you come up with such an unoriginal idea?

Sarah: Um, well, I was initially just trying to think of something to write for the inaugural issue of Alert Nerd's PDF 'zine, *Grok*. The theme was "pon farr," so I had this tiny, sleazy seed of an idea about someone who hadn't had sex in seven years. And then I also wanted to write a very specific character, an obsessive fangirl who has very absolute ideas about all kinds of geeky things, but is basically clueless when it comes to life stuff. From there, it just grew and grew and grew until I was filling up way more pages than I ever intended. As for the unoriginality...well, yes, I guess you could say that it's just like *every other* geek romantic comedy set at a comic book convention.

Braidbeard: Yeah, I'm totes sick of those—no offense. So Julie has a job that's sort of similar to one of your old gigs and she also has some opinions that are pretty close to yours and you kind of have the same hair or whatever. So my question is: is this really just your thinly-veiled fanfic about sleeping with a celebrity?

Sarah: First of all, we have totally different hair. I have *bangs*. Second...I mean, when I first started this, I was actively trying to avoid writing a character who was anything like me. She was even more extreme (read: mean) in the earlier drafts. But as this story developed, I started to realize that she was, in many ways, a version of who I was in my early to mid-twenties. I always had a theory about everything and I tended to close myself off from potential romances without even realizing it. So ultimately,

I understand her a lot more than I did at first, but I would like to stress: she is not me. This is not some sort of twisted autobiography.

Braidbeard: Reaaalllllllly? There's nothing in here that's even a little bit close to the truth?

Sarah: Well. I did have an, um, discussion with my husband once that sounded remarkably similar to the one Julie has with Jack about the whole Scott-Jean-Emma mess. But that's *it*.

Braidbeard: Whatevs, you and Julie are both completely wrong— FROSTLOPS is the best 'ship of all time and anyone who thinks otherwise is an idiot. But let's get back to the celeb angle. Why does she fall for a sort of famous guy? Why not just a regular dude?

Sarah: He *is* a regular dude—or that's what she figures out, anyway. Another geek culture type theme I was looking at was: can someone who has such inflexible ideas about everything change her mind? And that led to thinking about what she might be able to change her mind about within the context of the story. She has a very set idea about who Jack is and it's based almost entirely on the fact that she thinks he's miscast on some TV show. That just seemed like a fun, nerdy thing to explore.

Braidbeard: Okay, final question, 'cause I have to go update my Facebook status with my thoughts on the latest *Iron Man 2* stills. What do you think about the state of women in fandom today?

Sarah: Wow. That's actually...a good question?

Braidbeard: 'Cause I keep trying to score at cons and nothing's frakking working.

Sarah: I'm going to pretend like you didn't say the second part. I think it's impossible to deny that women are a huge part of sci-fi/fantasy and comic book fandom these days. I'm always shocked when people still assume all geeks are three-hundred-pound white guys who live in their moms' basements. For my part, I always felt like kind of an anomaly as a geek girl kid and that feeling continued into my first couple of nerd-centric jobs, wherein I was pretty much surrounded by guys. But the internet has been amazing as far as opening up that world and connecting me to other lady geeks and I feel like there's a lot of community being built there. If nothing else, I now know plenty of cool chicks who will readily jump into Scott-Jean-Emma debates with unabashed gusto. That's pretty fucking awesome.

One Con Glory
Playlist

"On Your Own," Blur
"Fuck and Run," Liz Phair
"Vanilla," Marian Call
"Don't Stop Believin'," *Glee* cast
"Surrender," Cheap Trick
"Promiscuous," Nelly Furtado/Timbaland
"When You Were Young," The Killers
"Lost in Your Eyes," Debbie Gibson
"Hey Julie," Fountains of Wayne
"Reno Dakota," Magnetic Fields
"One More Hour," Sleater-Kinney
"Black Hole," She & Him
"Ripchord," Rilo Kiley
"Now They'll Sleep," Belly
"Peace and Hate," The Submarines

Acknowledgments

Nicole Kristal, Sarah McKinley Oakes, Jenelle Riley, Matt Springer, Jeff Stolarcyk, Sarah Wolf, and Tom Wong offered delightfully insightful thoughts at various stages of *Glory*'s development. A girl couldn't ask for better—or geekier—friends.

Chris Stewart conceptualized and designed that pretty, pretty cover. He also named The Periodic Seven.

Max Riffner (page 3), Pj Perez (page 35), and Benjamin Birdie (page 67) created amazing art from my incoherent and overly verbose descriptions.

Janelle Tipton copyedited the shit out of the finished manuscript. I seem to use a lot of unnecessary hyphens.

Caroline Pruett, Jeff Lester, and Thea James made me blush with their incredibly kind words.

My family and friends—Kuhns, Chens, Coffeys, Millsies, and honorary Kuhn-Chen-Coffey-Millsies—continue to put up with my shenanigans. I don't really know why.

And Jeff Chen is just there for me every damn day. Thanks, honey—you're always welcome in my Cone of Shyness.

About the Author

Sarah Kuhn lives in Los Angeles with a geek husband, an extensive *Buffy* action figure collection, and way too many comic books. Her work has appeared in a bunch of nifty publications, including *Back Stage*, *Geek Monthly*, IGN.com, StarTrek.com, and *Creative Screenwriting*. As one fourth of the mighty Alert Nerd collective, she can often be found blogging about important issues (like the amazingness of Cyclops' hair) at AlertNerd.com.

CPSIA information can be obtained
at www.ICGtesting.com
Printed in the USA
LVHW111002300121
677895LV00034B/373